The Beaut

ANDREW

Adventures of the Little Owls (Part 1)

The Beautiful Witch

Illustrated by

A. A. GOODWILLIE

The Little Owl Gallery

www.thelittleowlgallery.co.uk

First Published in Great Britain by
The Little Owl Gallery
55 Harburn Avenue Deans Livingston
EH54 8NH

2013

ISBN 978-0-9926504-0-7

The Little Owl Gallery

Email : thelittleowlgallery@goodwillie.co.uk
Website: http//: www.thelittleowlgallery.co.uk

The Beautiful Witch

To Jean and Dave, Jan and Jem, and
our first Grandchild Ewan

also my mother who was always fond of birds

Thanks go to the following for their inspiration and
help

My models for the witches -
Sarah and Suzie from Axolotl Gallery
as well as Alexandra Lindesay
(None of whom are real witches as far as I know)

Edinburgh Zoo and the West Lothian Owl Sanctuary
who provided help and inspiration with their owls
as well as Bob Glover who recorded a real case of
Little owls living in an aeroplane
in an issue of the RSPB Birds magazine
which gave me the starting point for this little tale

Cherry Davidson and John Henley
for their editing and practical help and advice

as well as David Grosz
for his encouragement and support

CONTENTS

THE MAIN CHARACTERS OF OUR STORY

The Owls

 Jujube is our reluctant hero. He is a young Little Owl who lives with his mother, father and sister (Jubbly) in an old aeroplane at the edge of an abandoned aerodrome somewhere in the Land of Morvern. Jujube has many talents that he has yet to discover as he goes on our adventure. He would like to choose the name of Zeus (King of the Greek Gods) as his name when he becomes an adult, the other young owls find this a bit ridiculous, but as our story unfolds, maybe he will someday earn the right to such a noble name.

 Jubbly is Jujube's big sister, only just emerging from her egg seconds before him, and she, unlike Jujube, is very spirited and at times over confident although she does try to look after her younger brother she can be a bit bossy. She loves to sing and knows that she is very pretty so would love to call herself Venus (The Roman Goddess of Beauty and Love) when she has to choose her adult name..

Ginger is a young Scops Owl also living in the aeroplane with his parents. He is Jujube's best friend, but it has to be said that he is lazy and wants to call himself Morpheus (The Greek God of Sleep), much to Jubbly's disdain. Ginger, however, is loyal to his friends and will do all he can, not to let them down, no matter what Jubbly thinks of him.

Great Aunt Athene is a somewhat domineering character it has to be said. She is a Spectacled Owl and is by far the eldest female owl and therefor in charge of much of the owl organisation. Nothing gets past Great Aunt Athene who is quick to approve or disapprove of everything really. She is firm but fair, although she does seem a little ferocious to the little owls. She has never had a partner.

Thor (The Norse God of Thunder), sometimes known as Uncle Ivan is a Russian Eagle Owl. He is huge with an impressive wingspan. It is said that he is powerful enough to catch a comet and due to his expertise takes time off to teach the young owls each season the ways of the adult owls. He is greatly respected amongst the adults for his strength and prowess and has taught them all at some time. The young owls however believe some of the old owl's tales about Thor which we will not go into here.

Boreus (The Greek God of the North Wind) is the whitest and wisest of all the owls being a Snowy Owl. He too stands out due in part to his shimmering white feathers and his famed wisdom. The other owls always feel secure in his presence; although leadership can be a lonely burden he hides it well under his naturally calm exterior. He has a great strength of character and is unflappable under fire. Boreus is in love with Andromeda.

 Andromeda (Queen of the Night) is the most beautiful owl in the world and is an American Eagle Owl. She has unusual and strange duties which become clear as the story unfolds. She has feelings for Boreus, but tries not to make them obvious to the other owls.

 The Owl Prince, who is in fact, a human prince, was stolen from Forever Summer Island by Sylvia the Beautiful Witch, with the intention of using him for her spells..

If you would like to learn more about the characters and the types of owls that are used as illustrations in this tale then you can learn more by finding our website at www.thelittleowlgallery.co.uk

Snorky is a clever little mouse who befriends Ginger to escape being eaten by him.

 Elinor the mouse fairy – mouse fairies are never seen by the mice they protect. Nor can they be seen by other creatures. The Mouse fairy is able to protect the mouse with a cloak of invisibility at certain times of the day. The picture of Elinor with Snorky in the book has been taken using a special magic camera owned by the illustrator and is very rare.

 The fireflies are friends of all owls and appear often throughout the story. There has been a pact of friendship among the owls and the fireflies going back a long way. They will always help one another if they can, it is written into one another's code.

Sylvia the Beautiful Witch-it is enough to know that she may be beautiful, but her kind of beauty is but skin deep. There is a terrible secret to her beauty which threatens all the birds and animals in Morvern.

Artemis

Hi there,

My name is Artemis, but you can call me Arty. I do hope we are going to be good friends.

What was that? A very strange name I hear you say, perhaps, but I like my name, after all, I chose it myself after the Greek god of hunting and the moon. We owls like to choose grand names as our adult names. We particularly like the names that the Greeks and Romans gave to their gods. The Greeks and Romans thought that owls were particularly lucky. Because of this many humans still think we are lucky even today. I am not sure if I believe in luck or not myself,but many of us have charmed lives.

When I was born my mother and my father named me Chewy as all young owls are given a human sweetie name by their parents until they can choose a proper name for themselves. By the time we are adults we have learned everything we need to know, as you know owls are very wise and know much more about humans than humans know about us.

The story I am going to tell is about my special owl friends Jujube and Jubbly. You may think my tale is strange and mysterious, our world is certainly a little different from the way humans live, but I want to take you on an adventure into our world that will make you think differently about owls from now on.

I presume you can fly by now. What do you mean you "can't fly!"? Of course you can fly - you have an imagination haven't you? You can use that to fly with. One should always fly with imagination as Great Aunt Athene always said and she is a very wise owl. Yes you will meet her soon but, we are jumping ahead.

Before we start, I do realise that you are a very special person who likes secrets and wonderful adventures, you may want to tell your friends about the secrets I will reveal, but let's keep them to ourselves. Tell them if you enjoy the book but allow your friends to learn the secrets and enjoy the adventures for themselves.

See if you can find me in one of the pictures later in the story. Right? Come with me!

Wings ready?

Then strap them on!

Let's go!

The Beautiful Witch

CHAPTER ONE
Tripletree

Jujube and Jubbly were Little Owls, that is to say, they were born to Mr. and Mrs. Little Owl who lived in an old, broken-down aeroplane at the side of the airfield. It was a quiet place as no aeroplanes flew from there now and owls like to live in quiet, secret places.

They were not the only family living in the aeroplane. Mr. and Mrs. Scops Owl and their son, Ginger, also lived there.
The aeroplane, an old bomber, had crash landed after its last flight. Not long after, the War ended and the airfield had been closed.

The airfield itself was in a remote area where few people lived called Morvern. Morvern was a beautiful place of mountains and forest perfect for owls.

Jujube and Jubbly, the little owls, were brother and sister. Jubbly was older than Jujube, because she had started to break through her egg just three seconds before. Poor Jujube was always being reminded of this by his big sister. Jubbly had a habit of telling him off and this evening was no exception.

As she left the aeroplane she shouted. "Don't be late for Tripletree, Jujube. I am not going to hang around for you all evening." With a flutter of her wings she disappeared off into the soft evening light now settling on the airfield.

The outline of their aeroplane home could be seen against the half-light. The strange shapes of other old aircraft looked like giant birds sleeping around the edge of the field. None would ever fly again abandoned to nature long ago. Briar and knotweed tangled around the old aeroplanes now as the airfield gradually returned to the forest that had been there before. The owls' aeroplane home provided a dry and very comfortable place to live.

This was to be Jujube and Jubbly's first night at Tripletree. Jujube felt panic deep in his stomach. He was unprepared for Tripletree as well as being a little afraid of going there. Most of his life so far had been spent in the aeroplane with his family. Neither his mother nor his father would be with him, but his sister would look after him when they were there.

Mrs. Little Owl hoped that Jubbly would wait until they were all ready to go to Tripletree. On the other hand, she was pleased that Jubbly was confident enough to make her own way there.

In the centre of the woods was a very ancient tree, known to the owls as the Tripletree. No one really knew the age of the tree, but owls had been coming to the tree for at least a thousand years.

The tree was the very last of its kind in the Land of Morvern where the owls lived. The main trunk of the Tripletree was massive and twisting, with roots stretching out across the forest floor clinging like tentacles to the surrounding rocks and penetrating down to the deepest recesses underground.

Mosses and lichens, many as ancient as the tree, clung to the branches and roots, draping the tree in a bearded mist of silver green. Legions of small creatures scuttled about below in the dank mossy undergrowth, where a whole labyrinth of tunnels existed deep underground. The main trunk towered into the sky, branches spreading in all directions creating a large area of dampness and shade below the tree. Half way up the main trunk the tree supported another enormous branch, itself at least twice the size of any other tree in the forest. This huge branch turned skyward and behaved like the main tree trunk going vertically up reaching for the light. This in turn gave support to a final major branch which, in itself, was as big as any of the forest trees and gave the tree its name, the Tripletree.

The Tripletree stood out high above the rest of the forest overlooking the river which glistened like a great snake sliding through the forest in the moonlight. In this ancient and magical tree the young owls gathered.

Jujube and his mother approached the great tree standing with its crown in the stars. A great noise came from a cloud of young owls swirling around the Tripletree. Owls are often silent, solitary birds, particularly when they are hunting, but on this occasion they screeched and squealed as they excitedly flocked together around the tree.

Jujube said goodbye to his mother and flew in to sit with Jubbly and his friend Ginger who lived beside him in the aeroplane. Jujube was pleased that, for once, his sister did not scold him, as Jubbly had seen him arrive with their mother. They bunched up together on a big thick branch, sat quietly and waited.

The other young owls were flying in and settling around them. Some were playing about and still being a bit unruly. One older owl was checking to make sure that everyone was there and no one was missing.

The youngest owls, including Ginger, still had some baby fluff about them and looked a little lost. Ginger was the youngest there and had been the smallest of Mr. and Mrs. Scops Owl's litter. His older brothers had already fledged.

He was lucky to have survived really, as often the youngest owl did not. (It is rumoured amongst young owls that the larger owls in a litter will, sometimes, eat the youngest while the mother and father are not looking, but Jujube thinks this is just an old owl's tale and not to be believed.)

Ginger's first feathers were quite downy and made him look like a large ball of fluff. Eventually his down would disappear as his flight feathers would grow in.

When Jujube sat down alongside Ginger he asked him, "Have you noticed what's happening in the sky?"

Ginger looked up and saw for the first time a comet far far away. The comet barely showed, being a weak little star with an almost invisible tail. "Oh, so that's the comet my mother was talking about, she says it is going to be spectacular and fill the whole sky – doesn't seem much at the moment though."

Ginger and Jubbly sat watching and admiring this little wonder of the night sky, when Jubbly spoke. "I think it would be wonderful to wear a little comet around my neck. What a fine decoration it would make."

Jubbly continued, "It will be one of the most beautiful sights we will ever see, according to mother." She said this in a way that suggested that mother was always right.

Jujube and Ginger looked at each other and changing the subject talked quietly about Thor the Russian Eagle Owl who was going to teach them the ways of the owls.

Ginger whispered with a slight tremor in his voice, "Someone told me that Thor is strong enough to capture comets and has been known to eat little owls like us for breakfast."

"Don't be silly, our parents would not have brought us here if they had thought we would be eaten. I am sure we will be alright." suggested Jujube trying to hide his own doubts.

Jubbly did not help to convince poor Ginger when she said that she thought Ginger, being the plumpest, was the most likely to be eaten and that she thought this would give Jujube and Jubbly time to escape! Poor Ginger!

CHAPTER TWO

Thor

Suddenly a great shadow was cast upon the tree as a large owl descended out of the night sky to alight on the central branch.

"Wow, did you see that? It's Thor!" gulped Ginger who fell silent as the imposing owl looked his way. Thor said nothing for a moment before addressing the young owls in a deep powerful voice.

"My name is Thor, named after the god of thunder. I insist that is what you must call me when you address me."

"Phew, what a smell!" exclaimed Ginger, unable to stop himself as he caught a whiff of Thor's burnt feathers.

Ginger suddenly stopped talking when he realised that his comment to Jujube had been overheard by Thor, who was now looking down at him and glaring. Thor arched his shoulders then drew himself up to his full height. He now towered above Ginger and the other owls.

To say that Thor was impressive in his dark, almost black, plumage is an understatement. With his wings closed he was huge, even for a Russian Eagle Owl.

His clear orange and black eyes seemed to burn with an intense light and his sharp claws glistened with blood. Blood mingling with soot, was spattered all down his feathers partially covering a scorch mark which travelled all down his breast.

High above, on top of his head, striking black tattered ear tufts stood upright, his sharp beak formed a great arch and when it opened you could see inside where the rich red flesh of his mouth formed into a tongue which, when Ginger looked closely, flickered as a flame burning in the dark.

The fiery orange of Thor's stern eyes seemed to penetrate deep into Gingers' brain.

Ginger stepped backwards and steadied himself with a few flicks of his wings as he almost fell from his perch.

As he steadied himself flapping this way and that, he looked up again to find Thor hissing and opening his wings, which formed into a huge dark cloak casting a shadow over Ginger.

The tips of Thor's wings were burnt and ragged from his fiery encounters. This truly was an owl strong enough to catch a comet.

Ginger thought his end had come early. He was terrified and blurted out "I am sorry, sir." Not wanting to become breakfast.

Thor looked down at the insignificant little owl and then around at the other young owls that, by

this time, had scattered in all directions thinking that Ginger would be no more.

Some of the younger owls had raced along the branch away from Thor, diving into a hole in the Tripletree's trunk and were now cowering together for security. Ginger was hiding his head under his wings giving a perfect impression of a snowball, while Jujube and Jubbly had leapt away from him and were pretending to look the other way, frightened to make eye contact with Thor, in case they too might be gobbled up!

Ginger's heart was pounding in his chest and he could feel himself sweating under his feathers. He had said all that he could possibly have said in the situation. He just looked down at his feet and prayed that his end would be swift. The other owls could not bear to look and braced themselves for the worst............ which never came.

Fortunately for Ginger, Thor had already had his meal and simply decided to say nothing and moved on to more important matters.

Thor spoke again. "I will teach you many things over the next two weeks, how to hunt and how to find food, how to fly and make yourselves more acrobatic. You will learn how to become masters of the air and the forest, as well as how to carry yourselves as owls and make your parents proud to call you their own."

"You, young owl, look up! What is your name?" Thor turned and addressed Ginger in a great booming voice.

"GGGGG Ginger, sir." stuttered Ginger not quite believing that he was still alive.
His little knees were banging together so much so he could hardly stand up.

"Right Ginger, I will start with you and we will demonstrate the art of flying." boomed Thor.

Before Ginger could react, he seized Ginger in his huge talons and took off almost vertically. Effortlessly he lifted Ginger up. Tripletree dropped away rapidly below them until Ginger could hardly make out the surprised faces of the other owls, who were not quite sure if Thor had changed his mind about a meal. They ran out along the branch to observe Ginger and Thor who, by this time had ascended to a great height in the sky. They could, just about, be made out against a high cirrus cloud lit in the moonlight.

Despite the Tripletree's size, Ginger could hardly make out the tree below them, barely visible in the mist forming over the river. Ginger was now wide awake and wondering what was going to happen next. Thor folded his wings and

the pair plummeted towards the ground, the air
rushing faster and faster around them forcing
Ginger to half close his eyes.

The forest came rushing towards them. This alarmed Ginger who could not escape from Thor's tightening grip, stronger than the biggest bear hug in the forest. They were fast approaching the ground. Gripped by fear Ginger tried to scream, but could not, he could hardly breathe! Ginger was helpless and had to trust that Thor would pull out of the dive in time. The big tree came rushing up towards them. Flashing past the young owls at high speed they disappeared with a great puff of vapour as the cold mist engulfed them.

Thor pulled up and Ginger could feel his own weight pulling him towards the ground. Within moments they reappeared above the mist and were back up and onto the branch. The young owls screamed loudly and jumped from foot to foot as overjoyed owls do.

Thor called out to the thrilled young owls. " As you can see, there is going to be some excitement ahead, young Ginger here did very well and showed marked bravery, by remaining silent throughout, exactly as an owl should be, well done Ginger! Bravo!"

"Bravo!" he exclaimed again this time encouraging the young owls to join in, which they did, shouting and flapping their wings as they ducked up and down in excitement.

Ginger looked about him and checked that he still had all his feathers and working parts. He was shaking but, imagine being able to fly like that! My goodness that was brilliant! Was life at Tripletree going to be like this all the time he wondered?

Ginger was not so sure that he was brave, but he was pleased to be described as brave. After all Ginger did not choose to go with Thor remaining silent in Thor's tight grip. He was not about to disillusion Thor, or the others at this time. He decided never to laugh at Thor again hoping that Thor would forgive him. Ginger realised that much could be learned from this fantastic but scary owl.

The draft from Thor's wings had shaken the branches and rustled the leaves, as they plummeted past the young owls. It had been a bit of a shock, to say the least, as they had thought Ginger and Thor were doomed, until the two had miraculously reappeared swooping up on to the branch again. This demonstration of the art of plummeting left a very deep impression on the young owls.

Meanwhile Thor, rather pleased with his demonstration, decided that he would show them around the Tripletree and point out what made good eating.

The Tripletree supported many different creatures, everything from tiny insects and spiders, to grubs and moths, caterpillars, larvae, beetles, small birds, squirrels, a feast of yummy delights, if only one knew exactly where to look.

Thor was an expert in such things and soon they were discovering a variety of "numtious" things. Crevices in the trunk hid tasty bites, which the young owls found and enjoyed eating. The tree was so large that it would have taken weeks for them to find every creature living there.

Thor took them down to the forest floor where they went hunting amongst the autumn leaves to find voles and mice. Autumn was late this year, but already many of the woodland creatures were hiding away before winter arrived.

Countless leaves were changing colour, although this was not so obvious to the owls at night. The leaves were becoming brittle and falling off the trees in increasing numbers. Autumn and winter would make finding food a growing challenge, but there was still plenty to be found.

Ginger and Jujube wanted to taste everything, but owls' stomachs are not very big and they were soon complaining about being too full.

Until then the owls' doting parents had caught their food for them, but now they were catching their own food, how did they deal with a live mouse or hedgehog?

Ginger in particular, was finding it difficult to catch small mice and hoped that Thor would not notice. When Thor appeared Ginger pretended that he had managed a catch. Jujube had a spare mouse passing it on to Ginger, who had jumped on it just as Thor arrived. He pretended to struggle and then showed Thor the mouse. This had met with much approval from Thor.

Neither Ginger nor Jujube told Thor the truth. When Jubbly found out about the deception, she did not approve and told them so in no uncertain manner, but not in Thor's presence.

Thor demonstrated eating technique to Jubbly telling her forcefully, "I think it is important Jubbly that you try to gulp your meal down in one, if not, then at least gobble it down in as few gobbles as possible. That is the proper way for owls to eat."

Jubbly looked up at Thor and did consider saying to Thor that she thought that this kind of behaviour was unrefined, but thought better of it.

Jubbly remarked, "I find it difficult to gulp down large living creatures. I cannot get used to the feel of little things squirming and tickling around in my tummy."

"Owls cannot afford to be squeamish Jubbly. I am afraid you do have to kill them first before you eat them, that way they will not tickle." Thor tried to reassure her.

He decided to give a demonstration to the young owls of the proper way to hunt. Most owls do not fly around to find food. Owls living in the forest simply wait silently until food wanders along and then pounce.

At one point Thor showed how to wait in silence for a vole to come along then dropped dramatically from a height, with his talons open.

His talons snapped shut on the unsuspecting creature and instantly the vole was no more.

Thor threw the vole into the air catching it in his cavernous beak, gobbling it down while throwing his head back several times. The vole's tail disappeared in stages into the corner of Thor's mouth.

(I believe human children have a way of eating chips, that is more or less the same. I would be interested to know if chips wiggle in the tummy as they go down. I know voles do. - Artemis)

Jujube, Jubbly and Ginger practiced pouncing and catching over and over again, but Ginger had no luck in catching anything. They all found enough to eat and fell asleep on a branch to digest their meals – something which owls are naturally very good at. Any food owls cannot digest forms into little round balls called pellets in their tummies.

Jujube awoke some time later with a nudge from his sister who was already awake.

"Wake up Jujube! Thor wants us to cough up our pellets!" said Jubbly excitedly.

Thor looked along the line of young owls and said. "I want you in turn to show me how well you can cough up your pellets. I will award points for distance and style."

The young owls threw themselves into the contest and most of them managed to cough up their pellets well. The pellets sometimes "pinged" off the trees before disappearing into the mist above the river.

Moments later the sound of a gentle "plop" could be heard as the pellets entered the water below. Each successful "ping" and "plop" was greeted with much hooting from the young owls who thought this was great fun.

Jubbly thought she would be very discreet in her way of coughing up with hardly any "ping and no "plop", much to the disappointment of the other owls.

Jujube and Ginger, however, managed to get extra delight by coughing up together and watching as their pellets hit one another in mid-air with a "Splat!" The pellets broke up into a shower of pieces, "Ping! Ping! Ping! Ping!" they went as they bounced off the trees, before falling into the water, "Plopity! Plopity! Plopity! Plop!"

"Well done Jujube and Ginger! Well done! Spectacular! Spectacular!" shouted Thor. "Now that's the way to do it! Top Marks! I award you both extra Points!"

Anything else that Thor then said was drowned out by the hooting of the other owls.

Jubbly, who had been a bit embarrassed by the behaviour of Jujube and Ginger, was not amused by this at all!

Eventually Thor said, "That is enough for one night young owls, everyone has tried very hard and I cannot ask for more than that. Well done all of you! You had better be off home now!"

The little owls did not need any more prompting as it had been a long night and they were beginning to miss their families.

CHAPTER THREE

Home time

On their flight back to the aeroplane all of the owls crowded around Ginger to find out what it was like to have flown with Thor. Ginger boasted that it was much the same as when he normally flew, which impressed most of the owls, but not Jujube and Jubbly, who knew better.

Eventually all the other owls made it home except for Jujube, Jubbly and Ginger who had to fly a little longer until they reached their aeroplane home. When they arrived back at the aeroplane all they wanted to talk about was their night with the remarkable Thor. It turned out that their parents had all been taught by Thor who was very revered by the older owls who regarded Thor as one of the most daring of all owls.

Ginger decided that he had better not mention being in trouble or that he thought Thor was going to eat him at one point. He commented to his mother about the size of Thor's ears, but his mother told him that, the larger the ears on a Russian Eagle Owl, the more important the owl and that Ginger should not judge any owl by their looks alone.

Now the sun came sneaking up over the horizon and the owls suddenly felt sleepy and within a short time all were fast asleep. The sunlight filtered in through the cockpit windows and the dust in the air flickered forming a haze of golden particles floating everywhere. If the owls had been awake during the day, they would have realised just how much the countryside was changing. Autumn had taken hold from summer during the last few days.

The trees were turning red, gold and brown on their tops and formed a beautiful richly coloured patchwork which covered the land. The rivers were filling up as the autumn rains, falling on the mountains, were turning the rivers into torrents.

Soon winter would come, with its longer nights, which would allow more time for hunting, but there would be less around to eat. The owls had many things to learn and quickly.

CHAPTER FOUR
Flying

It took most of the first week at Tripletree for the young owls to learn to fly properly. Fortunately for Jujube and Jubbly they had fledged and could fly already. Ginger however, could not go too far from the Tripletree as he lacked some of the necessary flight feathers. He had to be rescued from various hedges, ditches filled with water and even branches which he had slid under on landing.

The other owls had not teased Ginger about this, as most of them were struggling a bit. By the second week however, nearly everyone had lost any signs of downy feathers and they were all making progress, including Ginger. They had practiced plummeting over the river as it was a little safer than doing it over the ground.

Thor taught them how to find their way around using the stars and the river, lakes and mountains as a guide. How to find food as the seasons change was another area of Thor's expertise.

The idea of seasons came as a bit of a surprise to the young owls, who had presumed that summer with its warm nights and plenty of food was going to be there forever.

The owls could feel it getting colder. One day Thor described snow to the young owls. Ginger found it hard to believe that the clouds could freeze and fall from the sky.

They ventured farther into the forest each day and noticed the changes in colour due to Mr. Frost creeping over the land each night. Looking up high in the sky, they could see Mr. Frost dancing in a circle around the moon.

Even the common insects were becoming scarce as they could no longer be found openly on the leaves.

The leaves were waving goodbye to the trees, each leaf making a final skydive into the sea of leaves on the forest floor, creating hiding places for the creatures who would hibernate there for the winter.

By the end of the second week Thor announced that Boreus, who was the oldest and wisest of the all the owls, would come to judge their flying ability. Each owl had to give a display of his or her flying skills ending with a daring plummet from a great height in the sky.

Thor was pleased with the way everyone was coming along. Jujube, Jubbly and Ginger were turning into really beautiful owls and very able silent fliers.

Thor's teaching of the Owl Code, which the owls had taken to heart, had by now made the young owls more respectful of one another. Thor had taught them that every owl had talents deep down inside, which made them all special. They should know that there would be times when bravery, boldness, or strength, was needed.

He had emphasised that intelligence, kindness and tenderness, were just as important qualities all important at different times in an owl's life. This had impressed Jujube as he had thought that Thor's life was all about being powerful and brave. It showed a completely different side of Thor altogether and even Jubbly was coming around to liking him.

Jubbly had also seen Thor's more tender side, despite her first impression of Thor being a bit fearsome. Ginger had also discovered Thor's kindness and patience for a young owl just learning to fly. His mother was right, it was wrong to judge on first impressions, good or bad.

According to the Owl Code owls should celebrate and respect their differences. Thor said that the owl world would be much poorer if all owls were the same.

Jujube had realised he would never be able to fly the way Thor could, Thor being such a big powerful owl. Jujube and his sister were only little owls and would remain so, but Thor had taught him and his sister that they too had special talents which they should try to make the most of. All owls were special, no matter what size.

Ginger had realised that he, being a Scops owl, had started to grow little ear tufts like his mother and father. He was now disappointed that he would not be able to grow ears as big as Thor's. His proper flying suit turned out to be very smart, however, maybe not up to Barn owl standard but pretty handsome just the same.

Thor flew the young owls over to the airfield where all the parent owls had gathered in the surrounding trees, which formed a wonderful grandstand for the display. The trees were lit by many fireflies who had gathered to watch the flying display. The fireflies and the owls were great friends, for reasons which will become apparent later.

Boreus had arrived and was conducting the proceedings from a prominent perch on top of the tail of one of the old aeroplanes. Boreus was a Snowy owl. Boreus seemed even whiter than snow, if that is possible, as his feathers had a beautiful shimmering quality when caught in the moonlight.

Boreus had none of the roughness of manner that was typical of Thor. He was strong and calm, with a voice that was mellow and full of the richness of years. His eyes were warm and seemed to inspire the young owls when he spoke.

His voice echoed across the open airfield and returned from the trees, where the adults were watching. Thor introduced each owl in turn. The young owls began their individual displays as Thor, Boreus and the adult owls looked on.

Boreus raised his wings to show whether each young owl had passed the test or not. It was impressive to see how the young owls had improved their skills in such a short period of time. Boreus was most complimentary and told Thor and the watching crowd of owls, that this was the best display they had seen in years, every young owl had passed with flying colours. The adults hooted and screeched as loud as they could to show their appreciation. They bobbed up and down on the branches as proud happy parent owls do.

Towards the end of the display Thor picked out Jujube, Jubbly and Ginger to put on a joint display. They soared over the airfield, coming swiftly at one another from opposite directions, showing off their hunting moves.

They raced off through the trees flying at high speed between the branches. Clumps of leaves would flutter in the air, as they flew fast and silent through the forest, to emerge into the open, flying in formation. They broke off and flew in spirals and loops over the airfield coming together again and again in a most dramatic way.

As one, they all soared up, breaking off at the top of their climb to come plummeting down. The owls watching caught their breath as the three broke away near the ground shooting off in different directions.

This was a sign to the other young owls that they should join in with their parents. They flew looping loops through loops finishing the display with a mass plummet.

Flying is such a joyful thing! Young and old joined together, plummeting and diving until the sun came up and the moon lay down to sleep.

CHAPTER FIVE

Catching Stars

The final week was given over to the art of catching shooting stars. Now, once you managed to get past the smell of singed feathers, it became obvious that Thor was a fantastic owl. He was big and powerful and it came as no surprise that he might well be able to catch comets. Have you ever tried to catch a comet? Comets come in all sizes and can be huge. The biggest comet can smash planets apart, according to Thor, and who would argue with him?

The young owls had gathered at the top of Tripletree ready for their first flight to the stars. Jubbly was particularly excited and was chattering away about the possibility of maybe bringing a shooting star home to keep in a jar she had found in the aeroplane. Jujube liked the idea, but wondered why their parents had not already done so.

Mr. Frost's fingers walked the branches as the clouds left the sky and headed down to sleep on the ground overnight.

Jubbly said to Jujube who was sitting on the branch next to her, " I think that the clouds like to fall asleep on the land overnight and when the morning light comes the sleepy clouds wake up and go on their way again."

Jubbly continued, "I have seen clouds hiding in the valleys, and sometimes I have seen them lying down on the hills. I suppose it's easier for them to move on in the morning when the sun rises and the wind gets up."

"Does the wind sleep at night?" asked Ginger.

"I am not sure if the wind sleeps anywhere as you cannot see it. It maybe just hides somewhere in the sky. I have heard it blowing at different times, but it can come and go in any direction and stop. I really don't understand the wind at all." replied Jubbly.

Jujube thought for a minute and said, "It is funny that Thor has never mentioned where the wind hides. He has taught us how to use the wind when it's there. Maybe we should ask him when he arrives."

At that moment there was a loud cry above them as Thor arrived and called to the young owls to follow him. There was a flurry of wings as all the young owls took off at once to join him in the sky.

Reaching the stars was going to be difficult for the owls. They were going to have to fly much higher than any of the owls had flown before. Flying upwards always takes more energy than flying level. They flew higher and higher encouraged and helped by Thor, who took each for a while on his back until they reached the region of sky where the shooting stars could be found.

Eventually they were surrounded by stars and earth and home seemed so far below them. They could see the curved surface of the earth lit up by the Aurora Borealis playing in the north.

Being this high in the sky, the owls were surrounded by stars sparkling brighter than diamonds. It was difficult to work out how far away the stars really were. Some were golden, others silver, many twinkled with the colours of the rainbow.

Thor flew them to a bright star which seemed to have a train of light flowing along behind it. They had to fly really fast to follow it. At first the small owls thought it may be a comet. Thor shouted that this was not a comet, comets were much larger. He told them it was a shooting star which was beginning to break up as it was coming near to the earth.

Everyone rushed after the star as little bits broke away in swirling showers of sparks. As it headed down it seemed to be gathering speed. Sparks were flying all around Jujube and Jubbly as they dived and Jubbly began to worry about her nice new feathers getting singed. The littlest owls were having difficulty keeping up so Thor suddenly reached out and seized the shooting star.

At that moment the sparks stopped and Thor spread his wings wide to slow down.

"Gather round! Gather round!" he commanded with his great booming voice.

The young owls slowed down immediately and gathered around Thor to see in his grasp a spluttering shooting star pulsing with light. It seemed alive like a beating heart but glowing with a glassy white light.

"This, is what we owls do, you know." he said, looking at their little faces glowing in the light of the pulsating star.

He had seen this look of wonder many times, but never tired of it. The first time catching stars is something that every young owl will remember always.

He continued speaking to his charges who were puffing and panting after their efforts, "We need thousands of stars every month to refill the moon as it runs out of light. It has no light of its own. We need to be able to see during the night when we are hunting, so the moon is a very important friend."

"We talk about a new moon, but it is the same old moon, it just runs out of light gradually and we refill it, until it becomes full again. We must catch enough shooting stars to refill the moon every month. The light from the shooting stars would be wasted otherwise. We will take this shooting star with any others you catch down to our secret valley tonight." said Thor not the slightest bit out of breath.

There was a sizzling of excitement which passed through all the little owls. They were at last going to see the secret valley all their parents had talked about.

Another shooting star raced past with Jujube and Jubbly's father chasing it. Their father and the star disappeared as fast as they had appeared.

"It's your turn now young owls, don't let me down, we will not return home tonight until everyone has managed to catch a shooting star." Thor called, "Be careful not to follow any star for too long as they do heat up and it then becomes difficult to hold on to them."

The young owls did not need a second bidding. They were rushing here, rushing there after the fast moving stars. After a little time the owls had managed to round up a number of small starlets, but Ginger and Jujube had had no luck at all.

The problem was that, most of the starlets that the young owls had caught were not particularly bright and Ginger and Jujube both wanted to catch something brighter. They hoped to impress Thor with their catch.

Suddenly, out of nowhere, a really bright star flashed between them. The star made a rushing swishing sound as it shimmered past. They set off immediately and gained speed as they started to chase after the brightening star.

Ginger tried hard, but could not keep up. Jujube tried harder and harder to catch up as more and more sparks showered around him he stretched out and stretched out. He could smell burning and hoped it was not his feathers.

Soon there were no other owls in sight and even the stars seemed so far above him. Finally he managed to draw level with the fast travelling star. He could feel the heat on his face. He reached out his talons and this time just managed to catch it.

Oooooooh!
Hot! Hot! Hot!

He could only just hold it in his claw tips, but he managed to hold it just the same. Thank goodness he had not taken it fully in his grasp. He stretched out his wings and slowed down, he could feel the star cool and, after a while, he could hold it properly, even now it seemed to tickle and tingle in a curious sort of way.

He looked deep into its glassy heart and he thought he could see another world and strange creatures living there. There seemed to be valleys and hills, rivers and seas, oceans filled with swirling light.

"Beautiful isn't it?" sounded Ginger's voice, as he flew up beside him. "See what's in mine."

Jujube turned around to see Ginger holding a red coloured star. They compared stars and Jujube could see a completely different world in Ginger's little red star there seemed to be even more little creatures swimming around.

"Is your star running out of light Ginger?" asked Jujube.

"No he has managed to catch a rare red star and you have done well to catch such a bright star Jujube, I can see you are both going to be good catchers of stars." beamed Thor who had come up behind them, "Well, it seems we have all caught our stars so let's take them down to the secret valley."

CHAPTER SIX
The Secret Valley

When they arrived at their destination the owls realised that there was no other way into the valley but from the air. The valley was completely surrounded by high hills, but could be clearly seen from the height they were flying at. They could not miss it as it was filled by a strange glowing light in the, otherwise, dark landscape of Morvern. The valley had many trees, which Jujube recognised as being similar to Tripletree. In the shadows below them he could just make out some tiny lights glowing there.

The valley floor had many hillocks and in many areas it was very rocky with escarpments and ridges, which would make it difficult to get about on foot. In the moonlight the frost sparkled on everything it touched giving the valley a dreamlike quality.

In the middle of the valley there appeared to be a lake. At first Jujube thought the lake was lit up by the moon, but as they drew closer he realised that the lake had an eerie glow all of its own.

The lake was overlooked by a number of steep sided hillocks. Some of the hillocks looked very unnatural as if they had been shaped by someone. A long gash had been cut into one of the hills and there were some signs of ancient habitation in the form of tumble down stones here and there, as well as, a stone circle on one of the nearby hills. The highest hill also had a peculiar hump on top.

The young owls were puzzled by what they saw as they had been brought up to believe that the valley was hidden from, and unknown to, humans. Did humans still live in the valley?

When they arrived the moon was getting lower in the sky and Thor told them to drop their stars into the lake which seemed to be radiating even more light by then. Many adult owls were doing the same, flying back up into the sky to catch yet more stars.

Jujube was reluctant to drop his star into the lake as he had hoped to keep his first one and take it home with him. However he did as he was told by Thor and flew in over the lake clutching his star.

He looked down to see a multitude of stars glowing below the surface of the lake as it streamed along beneath him. The stars seemed to be mixing together and all the millions of tiny creatures which each star contained were swimming around in a magical soup.

About halfway across the lake he decided to let go of his star, which sizzled as it entered the lake and joined its brother and sister stars. Jujube's star seemed to brighten when in the company of the other stars. Then it bubbled and dissolved and within moments Jujube could no longer make it out amongst its friends.

Ginger's star almost escaped the lake as it seemed to bounce several times across the surface before eventually breaking through and sinking.

Jubbly noticed that her starlet seemed to contain what could only be described as a dragon swimming in the light. How strange! No-one had seen a dragon for thousands of years. Dragons had died out long ago. Jubbly had assumed that dragons perhaps, never ever existed. They were mythical beasts, not real, but what her starlet contained could only be described as a dragon.

Jubbly dropped her starlet into the lake with a splash! She was a bit close to the surface of the lake and managed to get her feathers wet, which didn't please her a bit.

Thor called the young owls together and they settled in a nearby tree overlooking the scene. They were told to wait and watch. He thought they would all like to be there as something special was about to happen.

Jubbly joined the others and started to preen her wet feathers which seemed to have a slight glow to them after getting wet.

Jujube noticed he still had some star dust on his claws and decided to dust the feathers under his wings with this, rather than wash his claws in the lake. When Jujube opened his wings they now shimmered, much the same way as Jubbly now did all over. He decided that he would put the stardust in Jubbly's jar when he reached home. Surely no one would miss a little sparkling stardust?

Ginger looking out across the valley asked Thor, "Thor, are there any humans still living in the valley?"

Thor spoke quietly almost reverently for once. "Two tribes lived here once. One tribe lived in caves and mined the hills for materials which they used to make magic. The land around the lake had unusual layers of rock crystals filled with all kinds of magical elements which had something to do with the refilling of the moon. The mining reshaped much of the valley. Waste material was dumped forming mounds around the shores of the lake."

Thor continued, "The second tribe was a warrior tribe who always had fighting queens as their leaders. When their queens died they buried them up there on the hill overlooking the lake. The hill contains a burial chamber where the queens still lie. Unfortunately each tribe thought they were more important than the other tribe and they became rivals rather than friends."

Thor continued, "The tribe which used magic became more powerful and started to use it in selfish and wrong ways. The warrior tribe who had kept intruders out of the area and considered themselves the guardians of the valley also thought they had a right to rule the valley."

"They finally went to war with each other killing and fighting until only the warrior queen was left. Unfortunately the war left the valley a wasteland as far as humans were concerned and the queen took what was left of the magic ingredients departing from the valley by a pass high in the hills. Not long after, a major rock fall closed the pass. The valley became completely cut off from the outside world. After the humans had gone, we continued with our visits refilling the moon. No humans have ever come into the valley since then."

"Why am I glowing?" asked the worried Jubbly changing the subject.

"Do not worry little one, the effect is only temporary, it will wear off as soon as you dry out. The liquid in the lake has magic properties which it gets from the starlight. You have yet to learn that as owls, we also use magic, but only to do good deeds. Magic is dangerous in the wrong hands and must be used sparingly."

The moon seemed to be setting lower and lower in the sky and instead of disappearing over the horizon, much to the young owls' amazement, the moon became bigger and closer and finally landed gently in the lake sending out a slight ripple towards the shoreline.

The moon started to fill with light from the lake. At first there seemed to be only a trickle and then the sound increased as the trickle changed to a surge of rushing water and stars. The owls watched as the moon's seas filled up gradually and eventually the lake was empty.

The moon took off again giving a gentle sigh and hovered over the valley for a little while as its light strengthened.

More and more owls brought in stars and dropped them straight onto the moon's surface. Sometimes a loud crack could be heard, other times a sizzle and showers of sparks would flare up and into the sky, like the biggest firework display ever.

The moon itself started to hum and was seen to vibrate. Each time that starlight was added, huge flares of light would cascade around the valley silhouetting the trees and casting long shadows on the ground. The owls watched in awe from their safe vantage point in the tree. To the owls the moon seemed at once beautiful and majestic. The humming sound gradually died away leaving only silence. Eventually the moon serenely ascended up into the sky and soared effortlessly over the horizon leaving the valley in darkness.

The tiny lights that Jujube had noticed earlier seemed to be collecting together and could be seen meeting with one or two of the adult owls still returning with stars.

"Please Thor, what's happening over there?" asked Jujube.

"Any extra light the owls collect we pass on to our friends the fireflies. Owls long ago had agreed to give the fireflies some of the starlight in exchange for carrying out certain duties. We also have agreed to help one another when in difficulty." commented Thor.

The fireflies grew brighter and flew off looking from a distance like a bright silvery cloud, eventually disappearing over a hilltop. The adult owls gathered around the youngsters congratulating them on their first moon filling. They thanked Thor for his work teaching the young owls to catch stars.

The lake and valley were now dark. The moon had set behind the mountains leaving the stars still bright in the heavens above and the comet growing in strength a little each night.

The little owls now tired, started to yawn, so the parents picked up their offspring one by one and carried them home.

Jujube had many questions to ask his father about what they had seen in the stars. Jubbly remarked that she had also seen a dragon in her starlet and wondered if such creatures existed.

Their father had to admit that he had always wondered about this himself, but no one had ever been able to give him a proper explanation. He just knew that owls had fulfilled their duty to relight the moon for as long as anyone could remember.

There were some legends, of course, handed down by the elders and some day, when they had time and he was not so tired, he would try to remember the stories told by his own father and pass them on to Jujube and Jubbly.

"That's enough for tonight." said their mother, "It's about time we were home."

They flew out over the mountain tops and into the now familiar land of Morvern laid out as a black velvety carpet below them. They followed the river to their home, only just visible in the starlight. The little owls were almost asleep by the time they reached the airfield and their aeroplane home.

Jujube and Jubbly said goodnight to Ginger and soon settled down to sleep, but not until Jujube had filled Jubbly's little jar with the starlight he had hidden below his wings.

Jujube placed the jar of light near where they slept. It wasn't long before the sound of snoring owls could be heard wafting out over the airfield.

Morning crashed about as it tripped over the horizon waking all the creatures in the wood. Sunlight spilled out across the airfield.

Mr. Frost started to lift from the aeroplane wings his steamy, misty vapours seemed to contain the shapes of flying owls and shooting stars.

CHAPTER SEVEN
Singing Owls

The following evening when Jujube awoke he was surprised to see that his jar was empty. The starlight had disappeared! He complained to his mother that someone had stolen his stardust. His mother told him that stardust was delicate and did not last long after it had left the star. It had simply faded. He was disappointed as he had been hoping to make Jubbly a necklace in the shape of a comet from it.

His mother told him not to worry about the stardust and reminded him about the party.

"Run along to the tail of the aeroplane and practice singing with your sister." she told him.

Jujube eventually found Jubbly in the glazed turret at the rear of the aeroplane. You could see the whole airfield from there. The turret still had two large guns sticking out, very useful for sitting on. He could hear singing. There by one of the guns was Jubbly she stopped singing immediately Jujube appeared. He clambered up alongside her looking out to see if any of the other owls were around.

"At last here you are, I've been waiting for you to turn up Jujube. You should be practicing your singing as mummy asked us to! You know you must sing at the 'Questing' party!" scolded Jubbly.

Jujube sighed. Although Jubbly had a good voice for singing and would "Whooooo whooooo" at the drop of a feather, Jujube could only screech when he tried to sing.

"Aaaarck! Aaaarck!"

"Boy owls are not as good as girl owls at singing," said Jujube, looking down to his toes and wondered if they had grown since the last time he had looked.

"Rubbish!" said Jubbly "Mummy will be cross if you don't try like me. I have a lovely voice. Great Aunt Athene has said so and she is a very wise owl."

Oh dear, Great Aunt Athene, had made a strong impression on Jubbly. She was always right in Jubbly's eyes, so Jujube could not argue against that. Jubbly started to sing again.

"Whoooooooooooo whoooooooooooo."

Jujube closed his little owl ears which are hidden below his feathers and also closed his eyes but, no matter how hard he tried, he could not shut out the din. He decided that if he couldn't beat her he had better join her and sing, otherwise, he would never hear the end of it. He started to sing as loud as he could possibly go,

"Skraaaack! Screeeeeeeeek!"

His screeching completely drowned out his sister. She looked at him with a face like fizz.

"Jujube, if you are going to sing like that, then please go and sing elsewhere!"
Jujube knew that there was no way he was going to please his older sister and wandered off to find some of his friends.

CHAPTER EIGHT
Questing

Elsewhere in the aeroplane, preparations were well under way for the 'Questing'. The 'Questing' was a celebration which happened when young owls 'came of age' and turned into adults. The flying tests, the star catching tests and the singing test that was to come, would lead to the owls being sent on a quest. The quest was a final test before they became adults and were allowed to use their adult names.

Jujube brightened up when he found his old friend Ginger busy helping some of the other young owls in the cockpit of the plane.

Ginger and his friends were having fun decorating the inside of the aeroplane with fireflies that had arrived a few days before. There were plenty of old spiders' webs around for the fireflies to be hung upon and everything was beginning to look very colourful and bright.

"Hi Jujube!" shouted Ginger, "You've come at just the right time – we could use an extra beak. Here hold this!" Ginger passed him the little bundle of fireflies he had been holding.

Jujube became busy right away and picked out the brightest fireflies to light the cabin. Fireflies can be a bit naughty if they escape, so Jujube was very careful with his little basket of light.

The owls moved the webs around before placing the fireflies in their positions, trying to make sure each firefly was happy, because a happy firefly gives out twice the light. The fireflies did not mind doing this at this time of year as the owls always brought them fresh light from the shooting stars.

This kept the fireflies lit and owls always helped any fireflies who were in trouble.

Soon the entire aeroplane was decorated and looking splendid. The fireflies were more than happy and glowed lots of colours even some which have no names and humans cannot see. They glowed and glowed until they looked brighter than any fairy lights you have ever seen.

It was about then that Jubbly appeared looking for Jujube.

"Oh there you are Jujube. How dare you get lost! Mummy wants you to come straight away."

"Hi Jubbly," said Ginger.

"Lovely Jubbly to you," she said, using her 'superior' voice.

"Sorry Blubbery," Ginger replied with a grin.

"I think you're horrible," said Jubbly frowning as she fluttered away.

"Sorry about "Madam" Ginger. I think it is time to try on some of our costumes for the singing competition, so you had better come too."
The costumes were a little strange, but part of the trial. You see, when young owls come of age, they have to sing in front of all the grown-ups.

If the young owls do not pass the singing test they will not be allowed to use their adult names or to do grown-up things. Nor will they be given their stars either, but more of this later.

Part of the test was to make or find an interesting costume. Now, to be honest, owls are not much good at making things. "Finding" they are good at - especially in the dark, so most young

owls made do with things they found lying around. Humans were all too willing to throw rubbish about. So there was no possible shortage of things to make costumes from.

Ginger's favourite was an old funnel which he had found lying around inside the aeroplane. Jujube and Jubbly thought it was a very unusual choice and said so.

"I can always hide in it if they don't like my singing," Ginger commented, his voice echoing around in the funnel. He looked down at his feet which were the only parts of Ginger showing beneath the costume.

Jujube, worried about his singing, wished that he had thought of Ginger's idea first, but said nothing.

He thought he might fix it later, when he had more time.

Jubbly was too interested in her own costume to care. "I will be the star of the night," she told everyone, especially herself, as she wrapped herself up in an old orange peel she had found lying around.

She wore it like a scarf around her neck and Jujube wished he had made more of an effort as his costume was just a few extra feathers stuck around his head on a piece of tape he had found. The tape had lost most of its stickiness and kept falling off.

CHAPTER NINE

The Great Owls

For some time adult owls had been arriving from all over the Land of Morvern. They were looking forward to the celebrations.

Andromeda, an American Eagle Owl, had spent some time wandering the night sky picking out the prettiest stars to give to the young owls. The Milky Way has so many stars that it would take a lifetime to count them all and no-one ever did, besides, there were loads and loads and loads of stars lying around doing nothing anyway.

Andromeda could fly faster and higher than any other owl and was regarded as the real "Queen of the Night". She did not have the strength of Thor, but she could carry many stars at one time under her beautiful wings between the folds in her soft feathers. She lived by the Deep Lake, which, on silent nights reflected the sky perfectly.

Boreus had once written a poem for her about the lake and how he thought of her. She carries the poem in her heart.

If all we had was darkness
And stillness on deep waters
A million stars reflecting
A double universe of light
  Time now
             Time past
                        Time future
All present

I'd still pick you out amongst the stars

My constant shining light

No shooting star to flash and burn
No wandering star that will never learn

You are my Venus
                   My morning star

The brightest in my universe
The one I greet the day with..

Andromeda flew swift and true carrying her stars about the same time the young owls had set off for Tripletree, she had met up with Boreus the Snowy owl, whose name means "God of the North Wind".

Andromeda thought Boreus was very striking with his white feathers and powerful wings. He had been hunting below the "Northern Lights" which play and flicker in the sky above the North Pole. This is where the snow bear lives and the sun never rises for six months of the year.

Snowy owls can hunt day or night, although this is unusual for owls. It would be difficult if you could only hunt in the dark when half of the year is dark and the other half is light as at the North Pole.

Andromeda and Boreus met above the ice, flying over the Northern Ocean to arrive before the others.

Andromeda, when she arrived, went off to hide the stars, but Boreus had gone to Tripletree to meet with Thor and judge the flying contest. Boreus would also be in charge of the singing competition.

Mr and Mrs Eagle Owl, who lived close-by with their youngsters, and Mr and Mrs Scops Owl had brought their young owls out to meet Boreus. Great Aunt Athene had also turned up thinking it her duty to make sure all was well.

Jujube had thought it might be a good idea to take a picture of the scene, without telling anyone, using an old boxy thing, he had found one day in the aeroplane.

He and Ginger had been playing and had found this little box, which had a button on it. Jujube had accidentally stood on the button and there had been a

"FLASH!"

and magically a picture of Ginger had appeared from the bottom of the box!

His father had explained that the magic box that humans used was called a camera and he said to Jujube that he should not touch it as it may be dangerous.

Unfortunately Jujube does not always do as his father tells him and had told the other young owls that he had intended to take a picture when the adults arrived to meet them. What harm would it do to try it out, especially if he could record this very special moment?

Before Flash

Aunt Athene was busy introducing Boreus to the parents of the young owls who were wandering around outside the aeroplane, not quite sure what all the fuss was about. Boreus was a rather splendid owl and very distinguished looking, with his beautiful snowy white feathers and of course, Aunt Athene was out to impress him. She was just saying how well behaved all the young owls were in her care when suddenly, Jujube jumped out and pressed the button on the camera!
BOOMPH! The flash went off like a huge bolt of lightning. The youngest owls just about took off, but instead, they all bumped into one another in confusion. Mr and Mrs Eagle Owl scowled, Mr and Mrs Scops Owl fell over backwards with shock.

After Flash!

Poor Boreus looked as if he had been hit by a Wellington boot. Great Aunt Athene gave a look that would freeze a monkey on a stick.

It turns out that adult owls hate having their photographs taken. Jujube knew he was in real trouble and flew away as quickly as his little wings could carry him.

Great Aunt Athene had spotted him. There would be trouble. He went to his sitting gun in the turret to sit for a while and think what excuse he could make for his behaviour. It was not going to be easy, as he had disobeyed his father and upset the neighbours, and worst of all, he must have upset Boreus and Great Aunt Athene.

Every excuse he thought about only made him feel worse. Sometimes it is better to be brave and own up and that's just what he did. He waited until his father was home and told him all that had happened, what he had done and who he had upset and was very quickly in tears. His father knew Jujube had done wrong in disobeying him, but also knew that Jujube had done it with good intentions. Jujube had not realised how they would react.

So his father told him he must not do it again and that he would go and talk to everyone to put things right.

His father had laughed when Jujube had described Great Aunt Athene's face when the flash had gone off. Although his father did stop laughing when he caught sight of mother's face, which at that moment seemed to have a look very similar to Great Aunt Athene's as I recall.

Jujube's father explained to Jujube that adult owls dislike getting their photographs taken by photographers as they nearly always take them at night when owls are flying about and, of course, when the flash goes off they nearly always fly into something, as they are blinded by the flash.

Humans are often unthinking as far as owls are concerned. Nothing more was said at this point and Jujube went off to bed, glad that his sister had not been around when any of this had happened.

"Where have you been?" she asked when he snuggled up in the cold dawn. "Nowhere special," he replied and thought how nice it was to have a sister to keep him company. Although she could be a pain she did love and look after him and he loved her too, but would never say so, which is fairly typical of brother and sister owls.

The Sun began to stretch her wings over the horizon just as the little owls began to fall fast asleep.

CHAPTER TEN
Feasting

The following evening, preparations were well under way for the great feast. The guests had collected in the aeroplane's "Great Hall" as they called it. (Or bomb bay as the sign read, but no-one could work out what that meant.)

The humans had left a large round object in the middle of the aeroplane. There were lots of other pointy objects lying around, but none of the owls could work out what they were for.

This did not matter as the baby Eagle Owls, who had been too young to go to Tripletree, were already arguing over the first course of worms – I am sure you will all know that they are a very tasty bite.

Mmmmmmmmmm delicious!

Although a little rubbery a bit like octopus really. Tp! Tp! The good thing about worms is that you can stretch them out to make your meal last longer and if you like to play with your food there are lots of things you can do with worms.

Jujube's father who was a particularly brave owl for his size was much respected amongst the owls and had made amends for Jujube. Jujube was pleased as his favourite course was being flown in fresh.

Mmmmmmmmmmmmice! Tp! Tp!

You may not know this but, mice have little guardian angels. The guardian angels look after mice if they fall asleep during the day. Each angel has a cloak of invisibility which they can throw over the mouse, so that it cannot be seen out in the open. Unfortunately for mice, their mouse angels fall asleep at night, so the cloaks only work when the angels are awake during the day. Any mouse caught running around at night can end up as owl dinner I'm afraid.

Mmmmmmmmmmmmmmmmmm,

but they do taste nice, mice - a bit like raw chicken.

The feast quickly built up and included some particularly large hedge hogs – difficult to get into, but a great taste for those who like them. Snails get caught on your claws and slugs are a bit slimy and sticky, best to gulp the gloopy ones down in one, but beetles! Beetles are nice and crunchy and have a taste all of their own. Their black cloaks taste a bit like liquorice and the squishy insides a bit like turnip really.

Mmm Nium! Nium! Tp! Tp! Veeery Niiiice!

Thor had arrived with his wife. Few of the owls considered themselves important enough to speak to him as he was held in such high esteem.

Some of the owls were even frightened to speak his name he was held in such awe. Thor was looking forward to the new comet coming. It was quite a while since the last one had passed by and he had gone to wrestle it out of the sky.

Most nights he could be seen riding the biggest shooting stars across the heavens. His feathers were all black due to the burning stars.

He did not care about the soot. It was a sign of his bravery and strength. It has to be said that he did smell of burning, maybe that was the reason why the other owls although admiring his bravery, were reluctant to sit next to him – but please, if you ever meet him,

don't tell him that I said so!

His wife was a bit grumpy and did not seem to enjoy the meal and complained about everything – then again, I suppose, she would have to put up with the smell of singed feathers and things catching fire all the time at home. This must have been the reason for her grumpiness I suppose, but then again some owls are just grumpy and she was maybe just a grumpy owl.

Jujube's mother reminded them to gulp down their food as it would be rude not to in front of the elders. All good owls gulped down their food and then coughed up their pellets a short time after. Pellets never tasted as good on the way back up as they had done as food on the way down.

Jujube and Jubbly enjoyed their meal and played with the other young owls until it was midnight using one of the owl pellets as a football. By then, every owl they had ever seen, and more besides, had arrived for the competition and were busy coughing up pellets after a good meal.

At midnight when the moon was at its highest the young owls were called to make ready for the competition.

The owlets had all been asked to choose their adult names. Jujube had decided that he would be called-

Zeus – "King of the Gods"

The other owlets had laughed at him when he said Zeus, as he was the littlest of the owls.

"King of the Gods" indeed!

Jubbly had thought about calling herself Aphrodite, like her mother, but she had always found it difficult to say, so she decided on Venus instead, after all, the names meant the same. Venus means the "Goddess of Love and Beauty" enough said about her choice, I would say.

Ginger chose the name of Morpheus - the "God of Sleep and Dreams". He hoped he may become known as Morph, which seemed to suit him as his favourite place was his bed.

Something which Jujube had not thought about was the fact that the costumes and singing would be judged in alphabetical order and of course he had chosen-

zZZZEUS!

That meant that he was going to be the last one to take part in the competition!

CHAPTER ELEVEN

Competition

The time had at last arrived for the competition and Great Aunt Athene had organised everyone. The Panel of Judges included herself, Boreus and Thor, a very important panel indeed! The adult owls looked on as each young owl took to the singing spar and sang. A number of fireflies had been specially selected to light the performance area. Most of the other young owls taking part had done well and had been passed by the judges. By chance the last three owls in the competition were Ginger, Jubbly and finally Jujube.

Poor Jujube was wishing that he had put in the practice, but now it was too late. He also realised that he had no time to fix his costume either. Ohhh!

Ginger took to the spar in his costume and in a muffled voice he introduced himself.

"My name is Ginger and I am from the Scops Owl family," he could be heard to say under his funnel.

"I wish to be called Morpheus if I pass the tests."

He started to sing under the funnel and this gave a very strange sound, not like anything you've ever heard, really. It sounded something like the muted trumpeting of a swan, I would say,

"krawwwwwwewwwwwewwweaaaa".

Much to Jujube's amazement the Panel of Judges seemed most impressed. They seemed to like Ginger's costume and his singing. They had called it

"Artistic" and "Avant Guard"

whatever that means. So Ginger had passed! The fact that Ginger fell off the perch at the end due to him not being able to see properly, because of his costume, did not seem to matter, if anything it seemed to add to the drama of the experience.

It was now Jubbly's turn.

"Good luck Jubbly," whispered Jujube, as he helped her to wrap up in her orange hat and stole.

"Thanks Jujube," she said, "I'll be alright, but you really must try your very best if you are going to pass the test!" something Jujube really did <u>not</u> need reminding about.

Jubbly worked her way along the perch to the spotlight.

"My name is Jubbly and I am a member of the Little Owl family." She told the assembled owls. "I would like to be called Venus when I become an adult owl as my mother says I am the most beautiful of all the owls."

Aunt Athene gave a disapproving look at this point but said nothing. Jujube thought she did look striking under the fireflies with her bright orange costume which did bring out the very best in her feathers.

"Whoooooooooooooooo!
Whoooooooooooooooooooooo!"

Her notes went up and down and soft and loud in a very beautiful and delicious way for an owl to sing.

At the end of her performance everyone hooted in approval and the judges said that her performance was the best they had heard that night and quite beautiful for an owl - very operatic. Jubbly bowed and bowed and bowed and in the end it took Aunt Athene to go and haul her off the stage.

Jujube's moment had come and he shuffled along the spar, noting that the fireflies were not shining so brightly for him as they had used up most of their energy lighting Jubbly.

His voice was very quiet when he announced who he was.

"M-m-my name is Jujube a-a-a-and I am from, also, a member of the Little Owl family. I-I-I-I would like to be called Zeus when I grow up."

Some of his friends started to laugh and some of the adults started to join in, but Aunt Athene gave them a glare and it stopped. Jujube's knees were banging about like ducks dancing on jelly and when he tried to sing he hardly made a sound.

Aunt Athene shouted sternly

"Sing up boy!"

She startled him so much that his feather decorations fell from his head and at that moment he let out a   "Screeeeeech!"

which seemed to come from the bottom of his tail and then a

"Screeeeeeam!"

which filled the aeroplane and was so loud he could see the other owls flinch. He continued screeching and screaming at the top of his voice,

"Screeeeeeeeeeech!"
"Screeeeeeeeeeeeeeeeeeeeeam!"

When he stopped there was silence. Even Aunt Athene was dumbstruck.

Boreus looked towards Aunt Athene and Thor and finally at Jujube and said, "Young owl, that was the most fantastic piece of singing we have heard in a long, long time. It is exactly what a great owl's voice should be. It should ring out across the mountain tops or the frozen icy wastes. It should sound out through the forest deep, on the darkest night to let all creatures know, we are the kings of the forest. We also think it was a masterstroke that you started so humbly and dramatically threw off your headgear before singing in such a way."

"Wonderful! Wonderful!"

With that the owls hooted and screeched as loud as they could in approval of the young owl, who could not believe his luck. He caught sight of his mother and father in the crowd looking very proud and cheering with Jubbly and Ginger.

After the hooting died down Boreus announced that the young owls would receive their stars from Andromeda and that later in the ceremony Thor would issue the quests for the young owls to fulfil if they were to finally become adults and be known by their adult names.

Beautiful Andromeda gave out the stars, two to each of the small owls. The stars made very good landing lights, but more importantly gave the young owls magic powers which they could only use for good deeds.

Ginger's stars had a wonderful blue light and had been found reflecting in the lake and picked up by Andromeda. Jubbly picked out two ruby red ones as she said they would go with her eyes.

Jujube was given the brightest, whitest stars of all, as a mark of respect for his singing.

CHAPTER TWELVE

The Quest

After the owls had received their magic stars it was time for Thor to issue their quests. Thor addressed the owls. His eyes were fiery and he spoke dramatically in a very deep and smoky voice.

"We have heard that a young owl has been taken captive by a witch in the land of Morvern. We think the story is unlikely to be true as the Owl God, a long time ago, turned all the witches in the land into dead trees. We would like to find out however, if there is any truth in the rumour. As far as we know there are no owls missing. Unfortunately all the adult owls are very busy catching shooting stars at this time of the year and none can be spared to find out if the story has any truth in it at all.

You must go out and prove you can fend for yourselves as adult owls and return again by the next full moon. On your return you will be given your chosen adult names for good."

The young owls were told that they would leave at dusk the following evening after a good day's sleep. Different groups of young owls would be sent to various parts of Morvern and Jujube was pleased that Ginger had been chosen to go with him and perhaps he was a little less enthusiastic about having his sister with them, but he did not say so. He just hoped that she would not boss him around all the time on their adventure.

It was just about dawn when the young owls went to bed. The fireflies were really quite dim now as mother and father Little Owl rubbed their little beaks good-day as they settled to sleep and Jujube and Jubbly wondered what the following evening would bring as their mother sang them to sleep.

Sleep O sleep my babies
Sleep O sleep
The wind it runs its fickle fingers
Through the trees my babies
Through the trees

Leaves they sparkle in the moonlight as she
Wanders through the sky
The lake she lights and sees her face
Reflected with the stars my lovelies
Reflected with the stars

The stars will be your friends my angels
Stars will be your friends
When you are gone forget us not we'll
Love you still my angels
Love you still

Some night you will leave us babies
Some night soon
On swiftest wings you'll fly away
'Till then be still my babies
'Till then be still

Still be still my darlings
Still be still
No fox or wolf or wild wild witch will
Take you from us   still my darlings
Still be still

Sleep O sleep my babies
Sleep O sleep
The wind it runs its fickle fingers
Through the trees my babies
Through the trees

CHAPTER THIRTEEN

Adventure

The young owls had gathered outside the aeroplane surrounded by the elders as dusk turned to night. Each group of young owls was to search for the lost owl and Jujube, Jubbly and Ginger knew now that they were to fly to the Northern Forest in their search.

Jujube checked his stars were working properly looking under one wing at a time. Ginger was flapping his wings in a now you see them, now you don't, kind of way. Jubbly was assuring her mother that she would look after Jujube.

They looked up to the sky to see if they could see the North Star, Thor had taught them that this would guide them on their journey. Most of the other young owls were already on their way and had taken off in flights.

"Be off young owls." cried Boreus as they took off and circled around the aeroplane to say goodbye to their family and friends now disappearing far below them.

"Remember to preen your feathers properly." called mother, "Bye my little ones."

The owls were excited, this being their first time away from their families on their own, but they were also a little sad to be leaving their lovely aeroplane home.

Their parents tried not to let them see their little tears as adult owls are supposed to be very brave and not cry.

Following the North Star, they flew many hours before they came upon the edge of the great Northern Forest. Passing over the forest, Ginger noticed something strange.

"Why are there such a large number of dead trees below us?" he asked.

Jujube explained, "There used to be many witches here and the witches were nothing but trouble. Eventually the Owl God came to rid the land of witches turning them into dead trees. The Owl God only helps us in times of great need.

He is not cruel and has not destroyed the witches. My father says that the Owl God will someday restore them providing they have learned their lesson. He can only give us protection in Morvern as this is his land.

"Look at how many there were!" spluttered Ginger, looking down.

"Yes, this is where the final battle took place." said Jubbly who knew everything.

"Just as well there are no witches around now. I think we were just sent so that we could try out our wings and fend for ourselves using what we have learned. I really don't think they would have sent us out if they thought we might meet real witches, besides Thor said that there are no owls missing." continued Jubbly.

As they flew further north they noticed the moon seemed less bright and the stars seemed dimmer, how strange! They assumed, however, that this was maybe normal and that the stars may simply be brighter where they lived. Thor had said nothing about this. Fortunately, they could still see the North Star, although this too seemed to be losing some of its light. Flying over the forest, they had noticed fewer and fewer animals and birds about. The forest seemed to be somehow darker and emptier than they expected. They flew north all night until the first fingers of a cold dawn stretched out across the horizon grasping for the mountains.

"Better settle somewhere for the day." suggested Ginger who was beginning to feel really tired and a little hungry.

They found a large oak tree and settled on a branch deep inside the canopy of the tree.

They were lucky enough to find some insects to eat on the leaves. Ginger fell asleep and soon afterwards Jujube and Jubbly joined him, as they were also very tired.

When the sun came up, it stayed hidden behind the clouds. It started to rain and it continued all day. The rain fell heavily for some hours.

Each oak leaf bent under the drops of rain as they landed and formed into little rivers of watery sunlight running down the veins. Each leaf would overflow on to the next, until the rainwater fell to the ground. The soft pitta - pattering on the leaves was beginning to stop as evening came on.

It had been a very wet day and all the young owls could find to eat, when they awoke, were some green caterpillars. They would have been a bit tasteless if it had not been for an ant, which Ginger managed to find. If you squish an ant over your caterpillar they give off a nice vinegar flavour and add a bit of a crunch to the meal. Jujube doesn't like anything green, but ate his caterpillar chips up just the same. It was maybe going to be some time before they would eat again and he did not like the hungry empty feeling in his stomach.

They had made their promises, so preening came next. Preening is all part of being an owl and they spent some time making sure all their feathers were clean and in just the right place for flying.

Soon they were ready to set off again across the now darkening forest. Each night seemed to be getting darker, as they headed north. The moon and stars were even dimmer than the night before. Just as well owls have special sight which allows them to see well in the dark. This night happened to be the night before what human children call Halloween.

Flying high above them seemed to be a surprising number of what the owls took to be human aeroplanes, each flashing lights and making a swishing, roaring sound. They all seemed to be heading north for some reason. It was

difficult to judge just how high they were flying
above them. Some seemed to be surprisingly close,
but it was difficult to make them out against the
ever darkening sky.

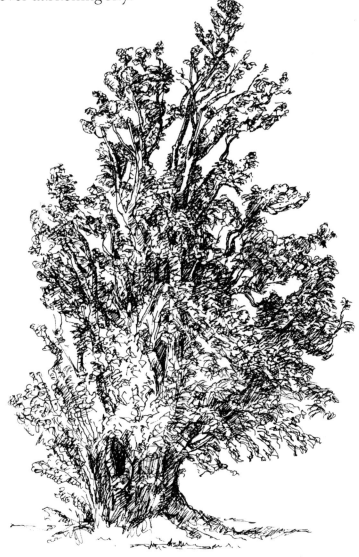

Chapter Fourteen

Separation

It was two hours after midnight when Ginger announced he was very tired and needing his bed. He was not used to having to fly so much.

"I don't believe in the witch's story anyway," he said settling on a pine branch, "Go on without me and tell me later what you find. I doubt if there is anything and I can't be bothered searching any more tonight."

Jubbly scolded him on his laziness and told him that he was an "Idle owl" and that they would carry on without him. They would continue to fly north. The comet seemed to be the only star amongst the dimming stars that was strengthening in the night sky. Jubbly hoped that Ginger would make an effort to catch up with them later.

"I think we would be better staying together Jubbly," pleaded Jujube.
"Don't tell me you're lazy as well! Call yourself Zeus! Come-on! Let him find his own way. He only needs to fly north. The forest will not go on for ever, it must end soon and then we can return." said Jubbly.

"Stay here if you must Ginger, we will stop at the edge of the forest. I am sure you will catch up and we will look out for you," Jujube said as the two owls flew off leaving Ginger on his own.

Ginger noticed a hole in the trunk of the tree and decided this may make a good hideaway for a while. You do have to be cautious with holes in trees as they may already be someone's home.

After careful looking, Ginger decided it would be all right to stay there for the rest of the night and day. It was a little damp and smelled of woodpecker chicks but the hole was a good size and not lived in for some time.

In fact, there seemed to be little living in the forest. The woods were silent, not the slightest sound, completely empty in fact. Ginger thought that it was strange, but Thor had told them that winter came earlier further north. After a while Ginger fell sound asleep in his hole.

It was a few minutes before dawn when Ginger awoke. His little tummy was empty now and Ginger looked around below the tree to find something to eat. Ginger was relieved to see movement in the grass below and pounced immediately.

He fell silently as he had been taught by Thor and flopped down on his first proper mouse hunt. Unfortunately he forgot to open his talons and had to scramble to get a grip on the mouse.

He lifted it up to his hole in the tree. He had been shown how to catch mice, but, of course, he had never caught one correctly on his own before. Every mouse he had ever seen was a dead one and this one was not dead. In fact it was talking to him!

"Pease don't eat me! Please don't eat me!"

squeaked the mouse. Ginger did not know what to do. Have you ever had your meal speak to you? The little mouse introduced himself as Snorky and said that he was trying to escape from the forest and that he would help Ginger to get out of the forest as well, providing he did not eat him.

Ginger asked him why they should be running away from the forest. The mouse told him that there was a witch who lived nearby and that she had been putting spells on the animals and that was the reason why the forest was so quiet. Ginger was not sure whether to believe the mouse or not, but the mention of the witch stopped him eating the poor mouse straight away, so he wrapped him up in some nesting material and looked around for something else to eat. A few beetles later and he was satisfied.

Ginger looked to where the sun was coming up and wondered whether he should trust the mouse. When he looked down to where the mouse was, or had been! No mouse!

He searched everywhere – The mouse had gone! Ginger could not understand and wished he had not been diverted. Had he just imagined a talking mouse?

Oh dear, no mouse and no meal. He was going to be hungry after all. Feeling a bit sorry for himself he settled down for the day and wished he was back in his nice warm aeroplane. What Ginger had not realised was that the mouse fairy had arrived at dawn throwing her cloak of invisibility over Snorky.

Snorky "Please don't eat me"

The invisible Snorky

Elinor, Snorky's Mouse Fairy

Ginger did not know about the fairies looking after the mice during the day, keeping them from harm if they fell asleep by covering them with a cloak of invisibility.

CHAPTER FIFTEEN

The Witch's House

Jujube and Jubbly had made good progress flying over the silent forest and had been surprised when they came upon a clearing that seemed to have its own moon lighting it. In the centre was a grand house surrounded by topiary trees.

Topiary trees are trees which have been cut by the gardener into all kinds of shapes. Jujube and Jubbly looked and saw many small trees trimmed to the shapes of birds and animals. There were deer, bears, rabbits and other forest animals in abundance as well as birds of all types, although, strangely, they could see no owls.

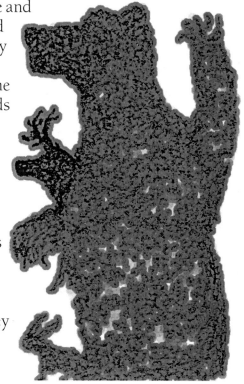

"Whoever lives here must love animals." remarked Jubbly. "Let's see if anyone is at home."

The house had high stone walls and many, many windows.

The owls found one of these open and landed on the window sill. Jujube and Jubbly looked into a grand hall with a high ceiling and large fire at one end and at the other end what seemed to be a very strange machine giving out sounds and moving pictures. The entire room was bathed in a bluish glow. Flushes of red and purple light ran through the walls of the room.

Sitting next to the machine was a beautiful young woman dressed in a long flowing white dress. She had long dark hair which cascaded over her shoulders like a waterfall containing a thousand rich dark colours. Her eyes were soft and as dark as the deepest pool. She seemed to be playing with the controls and singing in a voice that reminded the little owls of their own mother's voice, soft and gentle.

"Do you think she is the witch?" whispered Jujube.

"I don't think so, after all, mother always told me that I am the most beautiful owl in the world and I am very good, of course. I am sure no-one as beautiful could possibly be so horrible as to be a witch. Besides, her voice reminds me of mother and mother has a kind voice and would do no harm to anyone," Jubbly whispered back.

Jubbly flew off into the room and Jujube quickly followed her. The owls flew over to where

the beautiful woman was playing and settled down beside her. She stopped playing and the wonderfully strange music gently died away leaving a sound like a very quiet heartbeat which seemed to beating gently from within the walls of the room.

"Oh! Hello. What lovely owls! I don't think I have ever seen any owls in this part of the wood before. I do love birds and animals, and they are all very special," said the beautiful girl. The young woman continued "My name is Sylvia. Please tell me, what are your names and what brings you here?"

The owls told her of their quest to find the lost owl. She listened patiently and then told them that she would help them to find the owl using her special machine called a Topitron.

"You must be very hungry, stay here and I will get you something to eat," she said disappearing through a large wooden door into the room beyond.

Jujube looked at the controls of the Topitron and noticed that there were a number of moving pictures showing what seemed to be other rooms and the outside of the building. There were all sorts of pipes and wires leading off in all directions like the branches and roots of a tree.

He accidentally passed his beak through a light beam on the machine which made a loud noise.

This startled the two owls and they flew up to the high vaulted ceiling. "Why did you do that?"

questioned Jubbly, "You should not touch things that do not belong to you."

Jujube didn't answer. He was staring at the inside of the strange room. He could examine the ceiling and it seemed to have a pattern a bit like scales. The scales were shiny and iridescent, both brightly coloured and reflecting other colours at the same time.

A huge arch crossed the middle of the room holding up the ceiling. The arch had the texture of bone and pipes high above seemed to be playing the sounds coming from the Topitron. Steam puffed around the ceiling where Jujube could make out a pattern of vaults like huge wings. They were half hidden in the ascending vapours which seemed to cling and mingle around them giving the impression of breath on a frosty morning.

Sylvia returned with some food and laid it down below them on a table in the middle of the room.

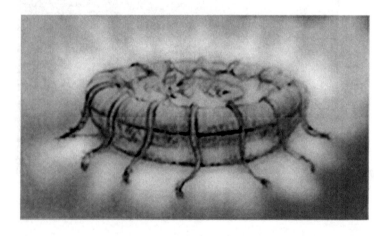

"Oh, there you are, don't be shy," Sylvia said looking up.

"I have prepared something very special for you, Mouse-taily Pie"

The owls, now very hungry, made straight for the food, and started to gobble their food down as good owls should. It was delicious and tasted of the very best mouse they had ever had. Sylvia suggested that she continue to play the Topitron while they were eating.

They listened quite enchanted by the strange music coming from the Topitron. It reminded them of home and their nice warm aeroplane. The sound captured the love of their families and the protection of their owl friends, it seemed to say "Stay here awhile, you are safe here, stay awhile stay in kind company. You need not travel any further, stay awhile and sleep gently little owls." The warmth of the fire, the music and what seemed like the best meal ever, meant that the owls were soon fast asleep.

CHAPTER SIXTEEN

Awakening

Elinor the mouse fairy tried all day to free Snorky, but had no luck. Ginger had tied him up far too tight. Ginger, being Ginger, had been asleep all day.

The light was beginning to fade as he awoke and the mouse fairy would have to go as soon as the sun disappeared over the horizon searching for her bed.

Snorky would have to decide what to do and quickly. He summoned up his deepest voice and said, "Master owl, master owl, do not be afraid. I am a magic creature and only appear to be a mouse. I will not harm you if you promise not to eat me." Ginger wondered where this mysterious dark voice was coming from. Was he imagining things, could this magic creature be the witch? He began to wonder – could this be the witch come to get him?

Oooooh, Nooooo!

"If you are the witch, please don't hurt me!" he screeched.

"I am not the witch but my powers are strong, you must promise to untie me if I reveal myself to you, if not, then you will be cursed for ever!" threatened Snorky, hoping Ginger would believe him and might let him go.

Ginger's little heart was quaking by now and he shouted out "Yes, yes, yes, I won't eat you I promise, I really do promise!"

Just at that the final ray of the sun disappeared over the horizon and the mouse became visible as his mouse angel fell asleep. Ginger was so impressed at seeing Snorky appear, that he did not question the fact that he had been so easy to catch in the first place.

Ginger rushed to untie him as soon as possible and noticed that Snorky did not smell like other mice he had eaten. He smelt more of flowers. At this point it is not clear who was more relieved, Snorky or Ginger.

"I am not a witch, but there is a witch living in this forest." announced Snorky, dusting himself down and trying to look relaxed. "I do hope you are not her friend?"

Ginger told Snorky no and then told him of the quest and about his friends Jujube and Jubbly, who had flown on and the fact that he was now missing them.

Snorky explained how he had escaped from the witch using his super mouse powers, but his companions had not.

He told Ginger that the witch queen had escaped during the great battle, before all the other witches were turned into trees by the Owl God.

She had gone to live with the warrior people in what was now the owl's secret valley, in time she had become their queen. This was before the battle between the two tribes.

When the battle had taken place between the two tribes she had been the only survivor and had made her way back quietly to the Northern Forest and her old home.

Rumour had it that for her to live there safely she had had to capture the last dragon living in the Northern Forest.

She had used her powerful stolen magic to do this, but no-one knew what had become of the dragon.

Over many years she had worked on her spells and had come up with two special ones. The first allowed her to free all the witches from the trees. The second spell was a beauty spell, which possibly meant that all the really beautiful women in the world were maybe witches. Snorky did not know if either spell was permanent.

He said that the witch had built a powerful machine called the Topitron which took the life from living things and turned them into topiary trees around her home. A tear came to his eyes as he described how his forest friends were lost to the Topitron and that is why so few creatures could now be found in this part of the forest.

Ginger thought about Jujube and Jubbly and wondered if they had suffered in the same way. Finally he asked "Will you help me find my owl friends, especially since your magic seems very powerful?"

Snorky seemed to hesitate but he replied, "I will take you there, but will go no further. Although my magic is powerful the witch is more powerful still. You must promise that we part company when we reach the witch's house and allow me to make my own way home."

Snorky did not want Ginger to realize, that he had no more powers than a mouse, nor did he want the witch to catch him.

Snorky hoped that Ginger would feel this deal was enough and maybe let him go, if not, he might escape later.

Ginger was a little disappointed his new ally would not promise any more, but was still glad that he had not been cursed by such a powerful creature and agreed to the bargain.

He gently picked up Snorky, putting him on his back before they set off. Snorky shouted commands to Ginger, as if he was some kind of wizard.

This gave Ginger more confidence in his new found friend and he flew on strongly towards the witch's house.

CHAPTER SEVENTEEN

Capture

Jujube and Jubbly awoke to the sound of an owl singing.

"Halloween and no one's here
I sit alone atop the stair
The wind it hisses through the shadows
The moon beams in the clouds

The witches sit and make their brew
Upon the ancient hangman's hill
Soon they'll go a-flying too
And cast their spells around

I'll take to wing and fly with them
For they are my only friends
A dreamer I amongst the stars
"The owl" it is my name

How long have I been an owl?
I know it's not for all my days
The witches took me for a son
A prince's life I had

My love she stands upon the tower
Wakened in the darkest hour
Knowing I still cry for her
And she still calls my name

And when I rest upon her hand
She with me will gently stand
"O gentle owl I love you still
Here amongst the stars."

I hope someday they'll break the spell
But witches' hearts are black as well
Am I condemned forever now?
To live amongst these stars?

Halloween and no one's here
Halloween and no one's here
Twit-twoo-woo woo woo woo wooooooo...

The sad voice died away and seemed to have come from somewhere up a long flight of stone stairs. The two owls were now fully awake and had discovered they were tethered inside a thorny cage.

The room where they were held had other cages and large sinewy roots ran everywhere connecting pieces of machinery. It was not immediately obvious to the owls that many of the knots in the wood contained eyes which were watching their every move. The walls seemed to be covered in blood red scales, how odd?

"So there is an owl after all, but he is not really an owl, he's a prince!" said Jujube.

"I thought it would be something like that all along." commented Jubbly, making out that she knew more than she did.

"It looks like you were wrong about the witch after all." Jujube commented, but Jubbly did not reply.

"We must get out of here and free the Prince." Jujube continued.

"And how do you suppose we do that?" asked Jubbly, who had been pulling at her tethers.

"By using our stars of course, do you not remember what Andromeda said to us when she gave them to us? We were to use them to do the right thing and we must work together. If we free the Prince and warn the others then surely we will be doing the right thing? It's not as if we are just doing it for ourselves."

The little owls opened their wings and revealed their stars. They found that, if they thought about good things, the stars shone brighter and beams of light came from them. It took a little time before they worked out just how to combine their beams of light and focus them on the tethers, but soon they were free and able to turn their attention to the catch on the cage. This they managed to open in no time at all, now they knew how to use their stars.

"Easy-peasy" exclaimed Jubbly as the cage opened. Hoping that it may be a while before the witch found out that they had escaped. They flew silently, as owls can, up the stairway to find the prince.

There he sat, in the form of an owl, looking out across the surrounding forest. They landed alongside him startling him in the process.

"Shhhhhhh!" exclaimed Jubbly. "We've come to rescue you."

"What's the point?" said the owl prince "I will have to stay here until the witch breaks the spell. I am a prince you know. I do not want to remain an owl for ever. No offence to owls, but I prefer to be a prince."

Jujube and Jubbly looked at one another and Jubbly said. "We can do magic using our stars, but I am not sure if they are powerful enough to turn you back into a prince. How did the witch manage it?"

The owl spoke quietly almost as if the witch could maybe hear them. "She used the Topitron, she can feed it spells and the Topitron seems to make them more powerful. It takes the energy from other living things just look at all the topiary animals outside."

"You mean that all these topiary creatures were alive once?" asked Jubbly looking out of the window down to the courtyard below.

"Yes, all she needs are some owls, like you, to complete the set and a small mouse which went missing; although she doesn't know yet that he has escaped. Using one of her horrible spells, she turned me into an owl, as she had not been able to find a real one. I know she is still looking for owls, because when she tried to change me using the Topitron it did not work. I think it can only work on the real thing. So I have been kept as a sort of witch's pet ever since. She still hopes to find two owls and I guess you are ideal", the owl prince sighed and added, "The food here is awful."

"GOT YOU!"

shouted the witch who had floated up behind them. They were caught for a second time and bundled off down to her dungeon.
"Now what's all this about the mouse?" she said as they disappeared down the darkness of the stair.

Chapter Eighteen

Witches

Soon the big house with the topiary garden came into view and Ginger landed in a large Scots pine tree at the edge of the clearing.

He and Snorky could see the topiary animals all around, but there was no sign of any owls, topiary or otherwise.

"Good," said Ginger "Jujube and Jubbly must still be fine."

The little mouse said "I will be leaving you now as this is as far as I will go." Before he could move however, there was a hovering sound above and Ginger froze when he realized that it was one of the flying machines that the owls had thought were aeroplanes. Now he could see it up close it appeared to have someone on board – was it the witch?

(Now if you have ever gone looking for owls in the dark, it is almost impossible to see them. If they are hiding in a tree, the patterns on their feathers suggest the dappled light you find on a tree's trunk, almost impossible to see, which is just as well, as the witch, who thought she had heard something, looked and looked, but could see nothing.)
Ginger closed his eyes and held his breath. After what seemed ages, the hovering machine moved off and he opened his eyes again. "That was a close thing Snorky" said Ginger "Look!"

There below them standing between the topiary trees seemed to be witches as far as Ginger's eyes could make out in the semi-dark. "Oh dear, which witch is the one we are looking for Snorky?"

"The beautiful one Ginger." was Snorky's reply. They looked and looked and looked, but there were

no really beautiful witches there. Most of them were still as ugly as turnips. The witches were all arguing about who had the best flying machine and were showing off with fancy flying displays and shooting spells at one another.

(Just for the fun of it one supposes, as witches have a very strange sense of fun.-Artemis)

One particular witch called Baobab, who liked to stand on her head, was enjoying turning the others outside in.

Yuck! This definitely took Ginger's mind off his
rumbling tummy for a while.
The other witches were squiggling around like
toothpaste being squeezed from a tube.

Suddenly there was a bright light hovering above the house and into the light stepped the beautiful witch with her shimmering white dress. This startled the other witches and they fell silent, not sure what to make of this beautiful young woman.

"Ladies, ladies, ladies thank you for coming," she spoke in a voice which was firm and clear.

"Oh isn't she la-di-da?" declared Baobab the witch, who had been enjoying turning the others inside out. The beautiful witch whispered something, which rushed around in the air swirling and zipping around the stone walls. It flashed around the witches and settled on Baobab's head.

Baobab let out a scream as she immediately turned back into a dead tree her arms became knotted and her fingers and thumbs elongated and twisted into branches.

More branches started to rush out from her chest and her hair twisted and turned this way and that forming creepers around her trunk. Her legs and the rest of her body seemed to turn into roots tearing their way down into the soil.

Soon pieces were cracking and falling off and holes began to appear in her crown and trunk , which made her look as if she had been dead for over a thousand seasons and had finally collapsed into a pile of broken branches. Baobab lay distorted, lifeless, crumpled and decayed upon the ground. The witches gasped remembering their time as dead trees.

"There will be no need for any further unpleasantness I am sure." said the beautiful witch. "That is providing, you will follow me and do exactly as I say." Sylvia threatened. "You are all here for your beauty treatment, on the most powerful night of the year, Halloween. We shall do more harm disguised as beautiful women. After all, who will suspect we are all nasty horrid witches, until it is too late."

The witches all laughed the way witches do, a sound a bit like sticks burning in a bonfire.

"The Topitron is all set up and ready and Ladies, I have finally found two gentle unsuspecting owls." A ripple of excitement flurried through the witches. "This will complete our set of creatures from the forest and complete the beauty spell I have for all of you. Their life force will be stolen from them and given to you,

"Because you're worth it!"

"Do we have to stay beautiful for ever?" asked a witch making her voice appear to come from her neighbour in case the beautiful Sylvia didn't like the question.

"Of course you do not, call yourself a witch and yet so stupid?"

With that the witch's unsuspecting neighbour was squashed by an elephant which had appeared suddenly, from nowhere, above her. The elephant, who moments before, had been calmly grazing on the plains of Africa had rapidly grasped it was too heavy to stay in the air and had only begun to ask itself why it was hovering there in the first place when it landed on the witch and flattened her into a flounder.

The elephant disappeared as quickly as it had come, returning to the African plains, probably wondering what had happened and if it had been 'just a dream'.

The flounder after a minute or two of discomfort flapped around and then popped back up, in a flippery flappery sort of way and returned to being the witch that had been there before. Several of the other witches were seen to gather closer around her as they rather liked the smell of rotten fish.

"What witch would want to be beautiful?" Sylvia exclaimed, "No, we can all return to being the evil, smelly, foul mouthed, ugly crones we love to be. When we have made Morvern ours again and I am again Queen of the Forest, you can do anything you want. Until then, obey me!" then she said darkly, "You really do not have a choice, as I can turn you back into dead trees again using just a single word."

The witches cowered as her words echoed off into the emptiness of the dark forest.

Ginger was at a loss as to what to do next, when he turned around Snorky had disappeared. Ginger's heart sank. He had hoped Snorky would have stayed around to use some of his magic power on the witches.

CHAPTER NINETEEN

Back Home

Mother Little Owl was beginning to feel worried as most of the young owls had already returned back home and had been asking for Jujube, Jubbly and Ginger, but there was no sign of the three. Mrs Scops Owl had also been worried and had asked the fireflies who were going back into the forest to look out for the three small owls. The fireflies promised they would journey north to look for them.

They talked to Boreus and the other adult owls. It seemed strange that none of the forest animals had seen the three companions around and that there seemed to be fewer animals to talk to.

When Aunt Athene returned from the forest the next night, she announced that she had talked to a deer who claimed that he had escaped from a witch. He had seen his two companions captured and that no-one would believe that there really was a witch living in the Northern Forest. Boreus decided that something had to be done..

CHAPTER TWENTY

The Topitron

The Topitron was an amazing machine. Machine is hardly the best description of such a unique beast. It is true that it formed part of Sylvia's house but behaved like some kind of animal. It was more than a machine to do Sylvia's bidding, it had roots heading out into the forest and connecting with all the topiary animals. It used their energy to give it life and sucked the light from the stars and moon and the sunlight during the day.

Most of the rooms in Sylvia's house were more like underground chambers in a complex of caves. Even the main hall seemed more like a cavern than a hall. Creepers and roots ran everywhere down the walls and across the floor.

Along the creepers there were groups of eyes watching everywhere within the house. Small screens and controls seemed to be in all the rooms and the balconies, even on the roof.

Deeply imbedded in the walls high above the main controls in the cavern was the living heart of a dragon.

This was the dragon who had lived happily in the Northern Forest, the last of his kind. It was he that Sylvia had used to build the Topitron. The thump of its beating heart could be felt in every room. Its skin had been used throughout the building to decorate the walls.

Bones were used everywhere to give the building strength and deep below ground its legs were used to hold up the structure of the dungeons where animals were kept until they could be changed into topiary.

The Topitron needed the life from other things to keep it alive. All the poor animals living in the surrounding forest had been captured and the life force taken from them. Sylvia needed at least two of each animal to make her major spells work. Their remains had, of course, ended up as topiary trees outside the house.

The Topitron, for some reason, did not like the light from the stars in the Milky Way. They seemed to cause it a problem as it would not work properly using their light.

Sylvia had locked up the owl prince and now brought out Jujube and Jubbly before the assembled witches. She tethered the owls to a stone plinth in the centre of the coven of witches. Pointing directly at the owls stood what appeared to be a glass cannon of considerable size.. Ginger could see that the barrel was connected to the Topitron by a series of pulsing cables.

Two mysterious blue lights appeared in the sky above and the witches were asked to gather together in the light. Ginger's mind was running fast what should he do?

Sylvia turned to the canon and switched the Topitron timer on. She took her place with the other witches. "Soon ladies we will all be beautiful and I will be the most beautiful of all."

Some of the witches scowled as they hated the idea of being beautiful and hated Sylvia all the more. The scowls turned to grins when they realised how much hatred they had for her. These witches hearts were full of hatred and that's just the way they liked them. Witches particularly like to hate their own leaders. I suppose they all think of themselves as superior.

The little owls puffed themselves up to look as big as they could. (Something all owls do when they are threatened and frightened.-Artemis)

They just stood there with their wings a little open and their stars just showing. There was a

"Whoosh"

as the Topitron started and the blue lights began to dazzle above.

The witches started to bathe in the blue light, as the air between the Topitron and the owls seemed to darken. The Topitron started to suck in their light energy which now pulsed up the barrel.

"Turn your stars on Jubbly. It's all we have left." shouted Jujube. The Stars had been brought by Andromeda from the Milky Way and when they lit up and the Topitron started to suck in the light, something very strange started to happen.

CHAPTER TWENTY ONE

Escape

Sylvia and the witches were so involved in what they were doing, they did not seem to realise there was anything wrong.

Ginger at this point decided to make his move. He flew down silently and stood next to the owls.

"Please free us Ginger. Switch on your stars and cut us free. Our stars are being used up by the Topitron and I am not sure how long they will last. You will need to focus your light and think of good things, please think of good things!" shouted Jubbly.

Ginger thought of his mother and how he loved her and missed her, but most of all he thought of her goodness. His blue stars twinkled and he crossed his light with theirs and dragged the light down through the ties. The birds were free in moments and Ginger pulled them away from the Topitron.

Something was going very wrong with the Topitron. Instead of the witches becoming more beautiful the spell seemed to be reversing and the witches were becoming even uglier.

Sylvia's beauty was fading fast and she was rapidly turning into the ugliest of all. There was a tremendous BANG! - as if something had failed deep inside the house and suddenly all the topiary trees turned back into birds and animals. They pulled up what remained of their roots and raced off into the forest.

The witches were quickly awakening from their enchantment and Sylvia turned to where the owls had been, but they too had fled. The witches seemed quite pleased with their new look, but Sylvia was blazing mad.

"Round them up! Round them up!" Sylvia screamed as the witches jumped on their flying machines and made off into the forest at break neck speed.

Meanwhile the owls had made for the room where they thought the owl Prince may be locked up and sure enough found him. Much to Ginger's surprise, there was Snorky and a whole bunch of fireflies!

"We've been trying to set him free," said Snorky, "but it has been too difficult for us."

"How come?" asked Ginger suspiciously, remembering Snorky's boast about being a powerful being.

"Let me out of here!" shouted the Prince.

All three owls focused their lights and the cage shattered around the owl Prince.

"Mind my feathers!" squeaked the owl Prince as bits of molten cage fell around him.

The owls raced to gather up the fireflies and Snorky stealing up and away from the witch's house. The fireflies switched off their lights, with the exception of one or two who mimicked the lights that the witches' flying machines had.

Ginger noticed that Snorky's ears vibrated and much to everyone's surprise made the same sound

as the witches' flying machines. This impressed
Ginger who thought it was just one of the special
things that Snorky was capable of, but it was just
one of these chance things that happen sometimes.
Snorky was not going to tell him that, however.

If any one of the witches had looked up at that
moment she would have thought that they were
just another flying witch. Certainly they made
good their escape, but maybe there was just so
much chaos below that no-one noticed.

The owls, Snorky and the fireflies flew swiftly
into the forest, far beyond the sounds of witches
rounding up the other birds and animals and
stopped in some tall trees on a hilltop. If the
witches were coming their way they could see
them from there.

"Oh dear this is all terrible, what shall we do?
The witches will soon have all the creatures
rounded up and the Topitron back working. Our
stars are beginning to fade and it will take time to
fly home and warn the others. What shall we do?"
repeated Ginger. "What about your special powers
Snorky?"

Snorky's head went down, "They only work in
daylight" he said.

"Oh." said Ginger wondering if he should
believe anything Snorky had said. He was
beginning to have his doubts, but after all, Snorky
had tried to rescue the owl Prince.

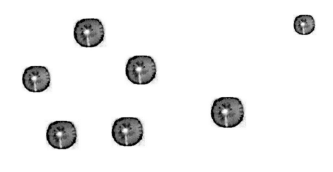

The fireflies had formed a huddle and were
talking animatedly to each other. Eventually one
of them spoke up. "We would like to make a
suggestion, if we may? If we give you the light we
have left could you use it to strengthen your stars?"

"I think so, after all, the adult owls bring you
light in their stars, it must be possible to transfer
the light back again." said Jujube.

After a little trial and error where one of the fireflies became red hot and lit up like a supernova (which is a special name for an exploding star).

The transfer of power took place and the owls realised that their power was almost back to normal. As the fireflies were more than happy to help, it seemed to double the power they were transferring.

"Now," said the firefly again, "we think you should try to contact the adult owls by singing to them."

"Don't be silly!" commented Jubbly, "None of us can sing as loud as that, not even Jujube."

"I hate to say this but she's right." said Jujube.

"Hold on you two, what if we used our starlight to focus the sound, maybe it would travel a long way, let's try it." suggested Ginger.

"What if it draws the witches' attention to us? What then?" Snorky asked.

"Don't worry just fly off south with the Prince and you will have some chance of escape. It will take us a little time to work out what to do." replied Ginger. The owl Prince and Snorky took off and flew south without delay.

The three owls gathered around and opened their wings. The fireflies suggested that they could use their bodies to direct the light and focused the light in a southwards direction.

Jubbly took charge, "On the count of three switch your lights on and focus, as soon as we are focused then sing as loud as you can, particularly you Jujube. One, two, three!"

A penetrating beam shot out from the forest and lit up the southern sky then moments later the owls' singing could be heard for hundreds of miles.

Moments later it stopped.

"What happened?" asked Ginger.

"I am afraid we are burnt out" replied the firefly, "we don't normally have to carry so much light through our bodies. We can still fly, but I am afraid our firefly lights may be gone for ever."

Would this be enough to bring the adult owls to their rescue? They looked at one another and wondered.

CHAPTER TWENTY TWO

Cats and Dungeons

It was not long before the witches rounded up all the forest creatures and netted up the three owls as well. The fireflies escaped the net and headed off south in the hope of meeting their other firefly brothers and sisters.

Sylvia had issued orders to take the stars from the owls when they were caught as she had realised by this time that their stars had something to do with the misfiring of the Topitron.

As the owls were flown in, it was obvious that there was still a certain amount of chaos. Various animals were being tied up and others were being put in cages.

This is also what happened to the owls, only this time there was a guard of Witches' cats.

Witches cats are not like normal cats. Normal cats see you as useful, if you are their owner, after all they get as much pampering and food as they want, but don't feel that they have to give very much back, unless they want to of course. Cats are very take it or leave it normally.

These witches' cats, however, are quite another thing. They love to be spiteful, they all hate other witches cats and are jealous of one another and grumble all the time they are together. They are only true to their own witch. Even when she is being very cruel to them they still remain true.

Each of the witches has a cat which she holds on to using a spell. This makes the cat do her bidding. They are not fed on things that cats enjoy to eat. They have to eat whatever or whoever witches just want to get rid of.

Witches love to turn small children into creepy crawlies and feed them to the cat so it is no wonder that witches cats get very crotchety at times. (Small children don't taste very nice, must be the talcum powder I guess – sticks in the teeth. -Artemis)

Each cat has to pretend to love their witch, but they hate them all the same - which of course pleases the witch all the more. Witches really are not very nice.

The three owls were feeling a bit sorry for themselves, and like the other animals, were taken down to the cellar to be locked up. The cats hissed and grumbled at one another as they locked up cage after cage full of animals, occasionally some of the thorns would catch in their paws and make the cats even more irritable.

The sound of key after key turning in the locks echoed in the dark cold dungeon. The sound was in contrast to the silence of the animals as they realised their fate. The first time the witch had caught them they did not know what it would be like to lose their freedom.

Now they knew what it was like not to be able to move, to live, to think and know freedom. The thought of being returned into their topiary state made them miserable. Some hung their heads in silence and others sobbed quietly when they thought about their fate.

The owls found themselves alongside some other strange looking birds and had decided to preen themselves as there was nothing else to do and besides it is what their parents had taught them.

The little owls had some hope, at least enough to start caring about themselves again, after all maybe the message had managed to get through.

Jujube imagined his father or Boreus hearing it and the owls coming to get them, but how would the owls be able to compete with the Topitron if it was working correctly? Would they even come in time? He began to have his doubts but did not say anything to the others, after all, what could three little owls do on their own?

After a while the other birds joined in the preening, knowing that their feathers would still

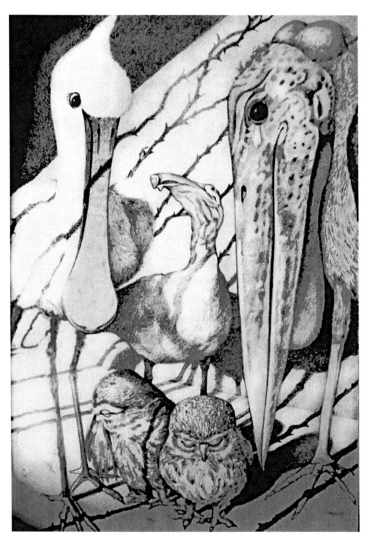

have to be in good condition, if they were ever able to escape that is.

After all the owls had helped them escape from the Topitron the first time. Maybe they could do it again.

The other animals seeing that the birds were preening themselves began to lick their wounds and quietly but definitely hope started to spread throughout the cages.

The cats, after all their exertions, started to fall asleep one by one until all that could be heard was the sound of the animals breathing in the semi-dark.

The owls noticed that they could only just hear the beating heart of the Topitron.

The Topitron was still there, but clearly not as strong as before. Its watching eyes seemed to be asleep for the time being, perhaps, that is why the cats had been put on guard - while the witches repaired the machine.

CHAPTER TWENTY THREE

Light in the North

Boreus had been thinking about the young owls and hearing the rumours, that maybe the witches had somehow escaped from the trees and that they would need the Owl God to come and help. He remembered only too well what it had been like during the days of the witches.

It had started with a little mischief, not all bad, in fact owls don't mind a little mischief as long as it is good hearted. As the witches developed their magic they had become very powerful but, also, had become more and more cruel. They even seemed to enjoy being cruel. They wanted to rule Morvern and had taken over, believing that nothing could stop them.

The other creatures that lived there were made slaves and after some terrible things had happened, the owls had asked the Owl God to intervene and clear Morvern of witches. It was then that the Owl God had come and turned the witches into dead trees to teach them a lesson.

Jujube and Jubbly's father had been out looking for them with the other owls, when the beam of light was seen in the northern sky. He heard their voices although they seemed a long way off. He hurried to Boreus and arrived as the other owls were flocking together in a huge circling flight in the sky.

"Boreus I have heard them, it really was them. I would recognise my young owls' voices anywhere!" their father shouted anxiously to Boreus.

"I am sure you are right, I am sure you are right. We have worked out the direction they called from and I have called the Owl God." assured Boreus, then he called to the other owls flying overhead, "Brave owls, the witches have returned and we must do what may be necessary to free our young owls. This will not be an easy task, there will be many dangers, so be ready and follow me."

With that he took to the air and a thousand wings followed him. They flew silently and fast to the north with only an occasional call from Boreus to keep them all on course. Boreus knew that a silent approach would be necessary for the success of their mission.

Andromeda flew close by, concealing the many stars in her wings. It took many hours of swift flying but, they found the spot where the owls had sent their message. For some reason the full moon did not seem to want to come with them and remained hidden beyond the eastern horizon. Looking down,Boreus was sure he saw a faint glow in the darkness of the forest.

Andromeda and Boreus flew down to discover a group of fireflies signalling to them. Some of the fireflies were unlit and told Boreus and Andromeda what had happened to the young owls. They also explained how they had burned their lights out trying to help raise the alarm. Some of the fireflies were crying as they believed that they would never be able to light up again.

Andromeda took pity on them and gave them some of her light. She held them gently in her wings and at first nothing happened, but then there was a faint glow from each of them. It was such a faint light but, just enough for the fireflies to see it. They gradually stopped crying and began to believe that maybe, just maybe, they were not completely burnt out after all.

They began to hum and as their hearts grew happier their lights began to glow brighter and brighter until you could see the smile on Andromeda's face. The fireflies danced out from under her wings and flew madly about as only fireflies do.

They thanked the owls and told them what had happened to Jujube, Jubbly and Ginger and promised they would direct them to the witch's house. They warned them about the Topitron and how the witches were using it for their own evil ends.

Boreus hid them in his wings and he and Andromeda joined the waiting owls to fly deeper into the forest and to the witch's lair. Boreus let out a high pitch screech, silent to our ears, which could only be heard by the Owl God. Boreus knew it may be some time, but the Owl God would help when he could.

Soon the feint outline of the witch's house appeared before them and the owls flew down silently in the darkness and gathered in the trees surrounding the house. The owls looked and looked with their brilliant night vision but, could see no guards, surely there must be guards?

CHAPTER TWENTY FOUR

Repairing the Topitron

Sylvia and the witches were going crazy. They were frantically trying to repair the Topitron which towered above them. They had gathered in the Great Hall where high above them, the dragon's beating heart seemed to be lacking power. If anything the heart seemed to be losing power.

Steam seemed to be escaping from all parts sometimes with a roar, forming a cloud, which drifted high up into the rafters. The screens, which normally gave such clear vision in and around the great house, were almost black and this is why the owls had not been noticed outside.

Sylvia had considered this the least of her worries at this moment and was ordering the other witches around. They were trying to use their combined witchcraft to repair the Topitron. The air was electric within the room. There was enough electricity escaping to make your hair stand on end and crackling lightning bolts were flying from one part of the machine to the other in a menacing way.

One of the witches went too close and there was an explosion. She was thrown to the other end of the room trailing smoke, with a zapping sort of sound.

There were screams and the smell of singed witch underwear. (Which it's best you don't know about really.-Artemis)

Balls of light would suddenly appear and float eerily about and then flicker away just as quickly.

Sylvia knew what was wrong. The only power that was driving the machine was the dragon's heart. For some reason the light from the moon and stars had been shorted out by the owl's starlight. This had allowed the life power from the animals and birds to seep back through their roots and led to their escape. All of this had had a bad effect on the Topitron.

The witches also seemed to be in trouble as some of them were beginning to turn back into dead trees, others seemed to be unable to get their spells working properly.

Sylvia used the controls to shut down any part that was not required including the Topitron's eyes and screens – after all, the cats were guarding everything, weren't they?

If she could stabilize the machine then maybe she could start feeding in the animals again to build up the energy required. It would be just a matter of time and a few witches lost here and there, after all she could free them again sometime in the future.

CHAPTER TWENTY FIVE

Break Out

There was a momentary flutter and an owl glided down to the house. Boreus had not given any order to attack. Why was one of his owls making such a move? All the owls watched as the single owl lifted off again in silence and flew back to the branch where Boreus stood surveying the scene.

Inside the dungeon, the cats were fast asleep. Jujube looked out from his cage and noticed what appeared to be a set of keys with two big ears attached approaching across the dusty floor. It was Snorky! He picked his way between the cats trying not to awaken them and made it to the cage.

"It's Snorky" whispered Jujube to the others, "and he has the keys!"

There was a slight sound of movement as all the other birds and animals tried to see what was going on. Snorky brought a finger to his lips and let out a gentle

"Shusssssssshhhhhhhh".

The cages were unlocked gradually, but no one moved until they were <u>all</u> unlocked and everyone ready to escape. Snorky had managed to get in through a mouse hole and told everyone that they would have to escape through the house – the only way out was through the Great Hall and that was where the witches were. If they all rushed at once there was a good chance that a good number would escape to where the owls were waiting outside to help carry them off.

Meanwhile Boreus was talking to the owl, who had risked giving their position away. The owl turned out to be the owl prince. He and Snorky had flown south and when they saw the large group of owls flying overhead had decided to join them.

Boreus soon realised that the prince and Snorky had returned to help their friends escape.

Boreus thought that the prince had been brave and had taken a big risk returning to the house to drop off Snorky. Fortunately no alarm had been raised as no one, not even the Topitron seemed to be aware of them. Boreus passed the word to wait and see if Snorky's plan would work. As soon as the first captives emerged they would swoop down and help.

Snorky crept back between the cats taking care not to trip over their whiskers and eventually he reached the one that was the farthest away from the escape door.

This particular cat looked to be the biggest in the room and Snorky looked up at its big fat face and beyond to the huge mound of fur that formed the body. When he had entered the room he had passed a mouse trap of the most horrible kind, the kind that normally comes with some cheese. He now manoeuvred the trap across the floor. Oh goodness! The smell of cheese was very tempting. It was even his favourite - Cheddar.

"Oooohohohohhhhhhh Nium! Nium! Nium!"

You could almost hear him thinking.
Suddenly it was all over, there was a **Snap!** and the cat awoke to find the mouse trap on its nose and Snorky standing there with his tongue out.

The cat was making such a loud

"Yeowwwwlll!!!"

that all the other cats awoke immediately and started to laugh at the sight of the cat prancing around trying to get the mousetrap off his nose.

They then caught sight of Snorky and all made a charge at once! Such fine food had not come their way for many months and they started to fight one another for the prize. Fur and tails and nails everywhere! The animals meanwhile made their escape up the stair. The cats did not at first notice and even when they did, they were so keen to get at Snorky that they made no attempt to catch them.

Snorky put on a good show until one of the cats managed to swipe him with her open claw catching him badly, knocking him into the mouse hole. He fell faster and faster through the air as the light coming down the mouse hole disappeared far above his head..

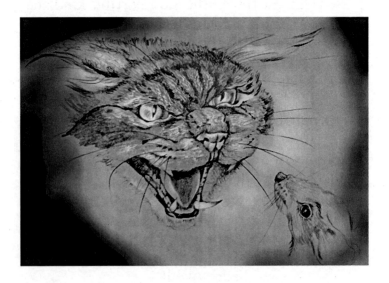

CHAPTER TWENTY SIX

Chaos in the Great Hall

The animals raced into the Great Hall much to the witches' surprise. Sylvia was now standing in the centre of the Hall in a trance like state trying to link her mind with that of the Topitron.

The remaining witches, not yet turned back into trees, dropped what they were doing and started to chase the animals around the Hall.

The goats and the bears, in particular were making it difficult for the witches to cast their spells. The goats butted the witches about and the bears hugged and hugged until the witches eyes nearly popped right out of their heads.

Some of the animals were making their escape through the main doors when Thor rushed in riding a huge shooting star. He let go and the star crashed with a blaze of light into the Topitron.

Pieces of the Topitron started to melt and burst into flames as other owls let fly with shooting stars which chased the witches around the room. The animals poured out of the building and made it to freedom and fresh air.

Boreus gave the command and the remaining owls swooped down from the trees and started to carry the animals off to safety. Boreus and Andromeda along with several of the more powerful owls flew down and entered the Hall.

It was a scene of disarray and carnage. Although the shooting stars were helping to confuse thewitches they were doing no real harm, far more chaos was being caused by the witches spells, which were flying in all directions and missing their targets, colliding off the walls and doing damage to the Topitron and the inside of the Hall.

The young owls raced over to Andromeda who passed them some new stars and told them to line up with Boreus and the others. There was so much confusion that the witches did not notice the owls standing in a line with their wings open.

There was a sudden burst of light as the owls thought of all the good things in the land of Morvern. Dappled sunlight falling through countless leaves, gentle streams of crystal clear water, full of tiny happy playful fishes. They remembered the hills and snow topped mountains glistening in the morning sun. They pictured the animals and birds joyful in their surroundings singing from the peace deep in their souls. They thought of their own life as owls in the Moonlit forest and the peace that was there and their happy family lives.

The light from their stars sheered through the thick atmosphere in the room and seemed to drive back the steam and smoke from the Topitron and the witches spells.

More and more animals rushed past and escaped as the witches, one by one, dropped into a deep sleep and started to take on the forms of dead trees again. The tips of their branches were catching fire and the black smoke from their burning made its way to Sylvia in the middle of the room. It swirled about her and seemed to be sucked in through her mouth.

Soon her hair and body were lost in the swirling smoke. The smoke seemed to turn into a black whirlwind around Silvia as she was sucked up into the Topitron's heart which now started to beat furiously.

With her sudden disappearance there came a terrific vibration, that seemed to come from the depths, the floor started to crack apart revealing deep roots. The sound of tearing metal could be heard as pieces of roof and walls were crashing down everywhere as the Topitron tore itself from the building. It started to walk on its roots as great wings sprouted from its back.

The owls, by now almost running out of light, rushed to escape with the last of the animals, now dashing quickly into the forest and heading off in all directions. There were no witches to stop them this time. The cats had come up from the dungeons and without the witches' spells holding them had decided to make their escape as well.

Boreus and the other owls flew up into the cool night air. The Hall by now was burning like a volcano. The roof fell in suddenly and created a huge flood of sparks to reveal the Topitron's head, part dragon, part Sylvia. Sylvia and the Topitron had merged!

She hauled herself into the air as the remains of the house collapsed with a roar. She was a mass of roots, thorns and scales, eyes seemingly everywhere. Her great wings formed glowing red sails as she took to the air and looked around for the meddlesome owls.

CHAPTER TWENTY SEVEN

Seeking Safety

The owls were beginning to panic all except Boreus.

"Follow me!" he screeched as he led them off to the east in the hope of finding the rising moon and some light. Sylvia chased after them. She was less manoeuvrable than the owls. The owls were diving and plummeting everywhere and were trying to distract her away from the escaping animals.

Owls are very good at plummeting but, they were beginning to run out of strength. They made for a patch of gathering light on the horizon in the hope that it might be help coming.

It was a very strange light that was forming there. It did not seem to be the usual light that you sometimes see before the moon rises.

As they flew closer they began to see that it was coming from millions and millions of stars massing on the horizon.

"Look!" called Andromeda "Look at the stars in the Milky Way!" Boreus shouted to Jujube "I do not have much voice left, Jujube. Call to the Owl God in your loudest voice and he will come to you."

" Do it now!"

Jujube did not need a second bidding. He let out a shriek that could be heard all over the land of Morvern and beyond.

They could see the stars from the Milky Way forming and reforming into the wings, body and head of a giant bird. Its wings spread out like a great city's lights filling the eastern horizon. It arose from the darkness and headed their way until it seemed to fill the whole sky. It was a wonderful mass of twinkling and shimmering light as it moved.

Sylvia was intent on destruction and was setting fire to the whole forest it seemed. The animals raced ahead of the flames and the owls were still doing their best to distract her.

The Owl God looked out over the burning landscape and drew in a deep breath. There came a great rushing sound across the forest, which blew out the fire as if it were no more than a candle.

Sylvia's many eyes had been searching downwards and on feeling the sudden rush of air she looked up to see the vast Owl God almost upon her. She turned and fled throwing fire and brimstone as she left but, this made no difference to the Owl God who chased her over the western horizon. A few moments later there was a sudden glow and distant rumble that sounded like thunder far off on a summer's day.

A long silence followed and then the moon started to slowly rise in the east, lighting the desolate scene below.

Eventually the owls gathered on the nearest tree, tired, but glad they had not lost anyone, although if it had not been for the Owl God who knew what would have happened.

"Is the Topitron dead?" asked Ginger.
"I hope so," said Jubbly in a very shaky voice "wasn't the Owl God fantastic!"

"Yes fantastic." said Jujube his eyes wide open and still staring in a westerly direction, his owl eyes reflecting the last of the fiery glow.

CHAPTER TWENTY EIGHT
Homecoming

Boreus said nothing, but turned and flew off south and the others wearily followed him. This was no quick flight home especially with the young owls, who took turns to ride on Andromeda's back. It was almost sunrise when they arrived at their aeroplane home and mother's warm wings.
Jujube's father had helped many of the animals to escape and had made his own way home. He had been told that his children had been seen flying home with Boreus and Andromeda. He was still relieved to see them there when he finally reached home. The rising sun was soon to out-do the moon setting in the west as the owls fell fast asleep.

After a long days rest the owls gathered around a circle of fireflies below the trees at the edge of the airfield. Dusk was gathering her velvet cloak around them. All the young owls had come with their parents and had been describing their adventures. None of the other owlets believed Jujube, Jubbly or Ginger when they told their extraordinary story.

Boreus called for silence and then spoke. "Owls, we are gathered here tonight for the naming ceremony and for the first time we will have the company of all the animals and birds of the forest."

At that there was movement in the trees as the deer, the bears and all the living forest creatures came out of the shadows and stood around.

"They asked if they could be invited to our naming ceremony, as they wanted to thank our young owls for the bravery they have shown in rescuing them from the witches. Although this is normally a secret ceremony and highly irregular, on this occasion I have given them my permission to come and on behalf of all the owls I welcome everyone".

Andromeda was asked to bless the owls' wings and each young owl flew a lap of honour showing off his stars and calling out his adult name as the other owls cheered. Finally it came the turn of Ginger, Jubbly and Jujube. "Come here my bravest little owls, little owls no more, after such adventures. Come into the light so that everyone can see you." The fireflies doubled their light and started to hum.

Boreus told everyone about what had happened and how the young owls had helped to save the forest and all of its creatures from Sylvia, the witches and the Topitron.

When he looked down at the three owls he was surprised to see they were in tears and asked, "What's wrong my little owls? Have I said something to upset you?

Please speak. I hope you are not hurt in any way after your dangerous adventures."

Jujube flicked away his tears and said, "There is nothing hurting our bodies Boreus, but our hearts are hurting deeply. We have lost two good friends along the way and if it had not been for them then maybe none of us would have survived. You see, there was an owl prince and a small mouse called Snorky who befriended Ginger, Jubbly and I. They came back to rescue us, putting their own lives in danger.

We fear that Snorky may have been eaten by the witches' cats and we do not see the owl prince in the gathering here and fear that he is also lost."

Boreus said "Look behind you Jujube, my friend."

Jujube and the other owls turned to where the fireflies were breaking up the circle and forming into two lines. They stared out into the dusk where the animals had parted to allow a young man to walk into the midst of the group. Although his feet were well lit by the fireflies his face was not so visible. He had an air about him, he was calm and gentle and not unlike the owl prince – of course - it was the owl prince!

All of the owls hooted and the young owls were so happy to see that he was alive and was no longer under the spell of the witch.

"Oh Prince! We are so happy to see you are alive. It's great that you have travelled here to meet us, but our little friend Snorky has gone, we think eaten by the witches' cats." said Ginger sadly.

"Who said the rotten old cats would get me?"

They recognised Snorky's squeaky little voice instantly, but where was he?

A moment later he popped his little head out of the Prince's top pocket. There was a sound which only comes from hungry owls at this moment and Snorky suddenly recognised that maybe this was not a particularly safe place to be in. After all, he was completely surrounded by owls! He dived back into the Prince's pocket.

"Protect me please!" Was his muffled cry.

"Keep back owls! Come out! Come out Snorky!" commanded Boreus, "No one will do you any harm, I guarantee it, otherwise they will have me to answer to. Young Ginger here told me of your bravery as we flew home and I am most impressed by what he said, a mouse of great powers I believe."

Snorky did not make a move.

"It is true we normally eat mice but, I will not dwell on that just now. I will give you a special honour which I alone am empowered to give. I am going to make you 'Special helper to the King of the Gods'."

There was still no movement from Snorky.

"You and all your descendants will for evermore be at peace with all owls everywhere. There will be no more eating of mice anywhere after such bravery."

Some of the owls were maybe not too sure about that idea, given how good mice are to eat but, no one spoke. An owl's word is his bond and if Boreus decides, then it has to be.

Snorky's nose and then his ears appeared above the lip of the Prince's pocket, his little eyes

twinkled and his smile followed instantly.
Everyone cheered.

"What about my friend the Prince and who is
this King of the Gods anyway?" asked the slightly
puzzled Snorky who had gone from possible meal
to 'Helper of the King' in a single bound.

"I don't ask for any privilege." spoke the Prince,
"It is enough for me to be free from Sylvia's spell
and to have lived the life of an owl for a while. I
have learned much from this. Being an owl has
taught me not to be so full of myself and to think
of others more."

"We shall help you get back to your land Prince.
We all wish to thank you for your help and
commend you on your own bravery. Can we ask
you, what is your proper name? We only know of
you as the Prince," asked Boreus looking at the
young man's face.

"My name, Boreus, is the Prince, that is what
everyone has called me all along and I am happy
with that. Boreus I am indebted to you and all your
brave owls."

There were cheers all around, especially
amongst the owls. The crowd became quiet again,
except for the Hoopoes who would not stop
hoopoeing around until they caught a glimpse of
Aunt Athene who was making her way towards
them.

Snorky had climbed down from the Prince's
pocket and was now standing with his three owl
friends. "Now Snorky, I would like you to meet
Morpheus that you know of as Ginger,

Venus also known as Jubbly and Zeus, of course
'King of the Gods." The three owls smiled and
Snorky smiled back with his best "I love Cheese"
smile.

The three owls received Andromeda's blessing
and flew around in circles overhead as the Prince
held Snorky high. The fireflies danced around in a
circle and everyone cheered including Aunt
Athene and the Hoopoes who carried on for hours
after, until everyone had stuffed some cheese in
their ears to get some peace.

The only ones to notice the small tears in Mr.
and Mrs. Little Owls' eyes were Mr. and Mrs. Scops
Owl who also realised their little owl had also
grown up.

The dancing and partying continued below the
moon and stars late into the night. They noticed
the comet for the first time in a while.

The comet was getting much stronger and
seemed higher in the sky. None of the owls, nor
the prince, knew how important the comet was
going to be in their lives, that would be for their
next adventure. For the moment it seemed simply
wondrous and magical this wandering beautiful
star.

Eventually the small owls flew up into the
branches as the other animals made their way
home to the sound of Hoopoes disappearing into
the distance.

The Prince had been given the small owls'
space in the aeroplane to sleep in until morning
and settled down there. In the tree above him, the
little owls fell asleep one by one, Morpheus, of

course, was first to go, then Venus who required her beauty sleep. Snorky also climbed the tree to be with his friends and was next to fall asleep, cuddling his invisible mouse angel.

Finally Zeus, the last to fall asleep, looked out and up to the stars. An adult owl now, he would carry his childhood with him always. He looked around at the others and wondered how their lives might change. He turned his face up to the sky again and there above him was the Milky Way, in the shape of an owl whose great pair of comforting wings stretched out, far across the midnight sky.

Vast and endless, eternal it seemed to him. He closed his eyes and was soon fast, fast asleep.

CHAPTER TWENTY NINE

Princely Worries

The owls had given the Prince a few days to recover after his ordeal. During this time Mr and Mrs Little Owl had been looking after the Prince who unfortunately, from the owls' point of view, had started to behave more like a human than an owl. He had gone from sleeping during the day to sleeping at night.

There was an overlap when they were all awake together and during this time the owls would bring him much to eat, but nothing seemed to suit him, not even the juiciest worms. He had tried his best to eat them, but the fact that they wriggled did put him off eating a bit. It seemed strange to the owls, as he had been quite happy to eat everything when he had been an owl.

When the owls asked him what he would really like to eat they were a bit puzzled. Could potatoes and carrots possibly exist? It seemed unlikely, especially when he explained that they had to be cooked over an open fire – how dangerous! Where would they find ice cream? – where would they be likely to find cows cold enough, even if they could milk them, and blancmange, was there such a thing as a blancmange tree? Human food is really strange!

At least he could still speak owl and make himself clear, but what if he ceased to remember the language? He was actually growing weaker by the day due to a lack of proper food. This was most worrying for the owls who felt that they had a duty to care for the Prince.

One day he went missing, the owls only realised when they woke up for their night time routine and found he was no longer lying in the aeroplane. There were a few minutes during which the owls panicked and flapped about looking for him. Everyone was woken up and the aeroplane searched from cockpit to tail plane.

"Let's see if he is outside Mummy", Venus said to her mother and flew out into the cold night air, quickly followed by the other owls. Morpheus and Zeus flew around in circles further and further away from the aeroplane hoping to find the Prince. It was Zeus's father who found him sitting by a fire cooking a meal.

The owls were called together and told to stay well clear of the fire as it was dangerous. Owls like most woodland creatures are fearful of fire spreading to the forest.

They sat with the Prince while he told them that he had appreciated all that they had tried to do for him, but from now on he was going to try to find his own food.

There was nothing particularly wrong with owl food, but it was not what he was used to in his human form. The owls did not like the look of the food, being cooked. Owls like their food raw. Cooked food makes them feel sick. Yuckitty! Yuckitty! Yuck!

Food that is still running about is their favourite, really.

The Prince promised to find his own food and to cook it well away from the aeroplane making sure the fire went nowhere near the forest. He still returned to the aeroplane to sleep, as it was getting colder.

The Prince was puzzled as there was only ever summer on Summer Island where he had come from. Plants flowered and grew fruit at all times in the year.

There was no winter season on Summer Island when everything seemed to die and yet that was what seemed to be happening in the land of Morvern.

He could sense the change to the cold air of winter and was glad that there were still some fruits and berries to eat. He particularly liked blackberries which dyed his fingers purple. His fingers still tasted fine long after the blackberries were finished. He would suck on his fingers if he was still feeling hungry.

CHAPTER THIRTY

Return of the Prince

The Prince had decided to try to sleep for the rest of the day after collecting enough food for his journey home. He wrapped it up carefully and put it in a bag, which seemed to be filled with a large silk sheet. He had found the bag and a few other useful bits and pieces, in the aeroplane.

He decided to keep the sheet as it may be useful to take with him as a temporary shelter. The bag was big enough to be able to carry many useful things including a compass, a knife and map.

He spent some time with the map, working out how to get home to Summer Island on the edge of the ocean. It was to the west of the Land of Morvern.

The island was quite large and very beautiful, with lush forests, mountains and streams that glinted in the sun. In many ways the island was unusual, as it only rained during the raining hour at night and had its own climate, being pleasantly warm at all times. There were no seasons there.

It was truly forever summer – the reason it was known as the Summer Island.

To the Prince it seemed a perfect place to live and he was missing it terribly.

Something the Prince had not noticed during his time with the owls was how quickly he was ageing. Clothes had replaced feathers when the witch's spell wore off, but much to his surprise he had started to age and grow hair in places no hair had grown before. He had quite a beard. His features were changing as he grew taller and broader to the point where his clothes no longer fitted him properly.

The owls did not have any use for mirrors, but one day when he had gone down to the stream for water, he caught a glimpse of himself and was quite shocked to see what he looked like. Even he could not understand why the change was happening so quickly. To the owls it was no surprise, hardly worth mentioning really, as owls grow up so fast.

He had been a boy for such a long time on Summer Island. It was a long time since he had been a baby, maybe hundreds of normal human years. He was aging rapidly now he was away from the influence of the island and this worried him. He knew the owls promised to return him home.

Evening settled upon the hills and looked down upon the airfield, in a warm sleepy sort of way. The comet looked beautiful in the evening light and now appeared before any of the stars, including the evening star.

The Prince would ask the owls to help him return as soon as they were awake.

Although the Prince enjoyed the owls company he was feeling homesick and wished to return home to Summer Island.

Neither the Prince nor the owls realised the dangers they would face as he returned home. The peaceful and beautiful Summer Island had changed since the Prince had been taken from it by Sylvia the witch. What of Sylvia and the Topitron? They had been chased out of Morvern, but where had they gone? What of the approaching comet? The Prince and the owls had no idea just how much it would change their lives - continue the adventure in the next book of the series "The Return of the Prince." Until then there are many enjoyable things to do on our website at www.thelittleowlgallery.co.uk including things to make and bake, songs, stories, real owl stuff and news, so please join me there

I do hope you have enjoyed the story so far and will join me in our next adventure. "The Return of the Prince"

'Bye for now!

Your friend Artemis

A word from the author and illustrator.

Books have a strange way of coming about, this one started when I found an article and photographs by Bob Glover in the RSPB magazine on an owl family who set up home in an aeroplane. About the same time my friend John Henley asked me to draw some owls and when I became involved I developed an interest in these mysterious and beautiful birds.

Some years later I was preparing work for an exhibition in the Axolotl Gallery run by Sarah Wilson when she asked me if I had more of the owl drawings and paintings and suggested that I make them a major part of my exhibition. Sarah and her friend Suzie were so enthusiastic that they suggested writing a book based on the pictures. So I sat down and wrote a few chapters and thought it may be a good idea to try out some of the story on those who were likely to enjoy such a thing. So two children's days were organised for local schools and I went out and bought some trees for the inside of the gallery.

Edinburgh Zoo, when asked, sent along a couple of beautiful owls with their keepers who taught the children about real owls. Eventually Sarah and Suzie along with my model Alexandra Lindesay made it into the book as witches.

During the exhibition I read chapters of the book and did some drawing with the children and a great time was had by all! John Henley and Cherry Davidson very kindly edited what I had written and

David Grosz gave his encouragement and permission to use one of my landscape paintings which he now owns, of the secret valley.

Being interested in songwriting and poetry I thought I would include a few in the story and if you want to hear sung versions of the songs you will find them on the website at

www. thelittleowlgallery.co.uk

The songs use traditional tunes although I have written the lyrics. I hope you enjoy them as well as the book.

My own wife and children have been a source of happiness in my family life and many moments from this have been used as well as characters in my teaching and childhood lives.

So to one and all I would like to say thank you, because without everyone involved this book would never have made it on to the page. I apologise for any faults or inaccuracies and state that they are purely my own.   A.A.

Look for us all on
THE LITTLE OWL GALLERY
website at
www.thelittleowlgallery.co.uk
Copies of this book and further books in the series
can be ordered on our website and supplied
directly to you. There is also a large coloured
version of the book available directly from us.

Why not join our mailing list for news of further
publications? On our website you will find:

Ideas for Owl Halloween Parties

Games and Masks / Recipes for Owl Food /Songs
and Poetry / Pictures and Photographs
Real Owl stuff / A Children's Play /News

Lightning Source UK Ltd.
Milton Keynes UK
UKOW04f1408171113

221246UK00001B/1/P